Elliott,

My homie, You are
a rare breed. Keep
doing what cha do!
Much Luv

May many Blessings to
You & your family!

Thanks for your support!

8-20-19

THREE FRIENDS . . . THE PERFECT STEREOTYPE

ANTHONY S.

Fulton Books, Inc.
Meadville, PA

First originally published by Fulton Books 2017

ISBN 978-1-63338-633-4 (Paperback)
ISBN 978-1-63338-756-0 (Hardcover)
ISBN 978-1-63338-634-1 (Digital)

Printed in the United States of America

ACKNOWLEDGMENTS

I would like to thank the following people who have inspired me or have been a part of my Life.

Our Creator/Father in Heaven, Jesus Christ our Redeemer, My Dad "Jake" (RIP), My Mom Datie "Dee", My Wife Cheryl (Cricket), My wonderful Children…Charnell, Marvin and Toniqua. My Grandchildren…. Israel & Immanuel. My Sister Stephanie (Duffy), My Brother's Cliff, Rodney, & Yancy D., Kimberla Lawson Roby, Christina (Coco), Mr. & Mrs. Felix Williams (In-Laws), Mr. & Mrs. Anthony O'Neal, Mr. & Mrs. Derrick Jones, Sr., Mr. & Mrs. Derrick Jones, Jr., Mr. & Mrs. Bobby Griffin, Felix (Bone), Mr. & Mrs. Ricky Jones "Wock", My Step-mom Betty, My God-mom Mama Millicent, Mr. & Mrs. Johnnie Lipkin (Blaze), Aunt Sheron & Florinda (Flo), Mr. & Mrs. Brian Holt, Mr. Holt, Mr. & Mrs. Nick Lamb, Mr. & Mrs. Walter Conwell, Eric & Elroy (Goodman), Natalie (Sis), Ojwan & Mingnon Jiles, Vince Adams, Sidney W. (Dope), Mr. & Mrs. Marlon Jones, Big Woo, Corey, Elliott, "E", "Ant", Big Joe, Mr. & Mrs. Jeff Edwards, "Unknown", The "Club", Mr. & Mrs. Jim Baker. Peace Church Family, Aunt "Bee", "Vamp", Vianne (cuz) Zena (cuz), Tia (cuz), Mr. & Mrs. Carl Green, Olen Bell, Scott Green, Big Tim (Dogg), James Kidd, Mrs. Kidd, Peggy Kidd, Squishi (Lil sis) & Terry…Terry Mills & family, Mr. & Mrs. Robert Nealy, Mr. & Mrs. Adrian Golden, Dione ("D") Golden, Ferrell G. & family, Darrel G. & family, "Dee"

George. "Trish"(cuz), Angel (cuz), Aunt Liz, Aunt Connie, Mr. & Mrs. Don Jones & family, Paul Cannon & family, Uncle Neotha & family, Kev & Ouida, "Shell", Paulette, Whitney & Robin, Shakur, Paulanne (sis-in-law), "Big Mike", Darrel C. (Smooth), Laray J., Robert P. (Jr.), Donald (Stamp), K.D., Judge (Jug Head), Jackie McFadden, Deena (cuz), Dana (cuz), John D. (cuz), Flo (cuz), Kelly B. (cuz) (RIP), Crazy Toones (RIP), Dub C., Tracy & Lisa Parker (cuz), Mr. & Mrs. Rodney Johnson, Mr. & Mrs. Norman Johnson, Mr. & Mrs. Gordon, Ken & Dominique, Chrystal (God Daughter), James Madden & family, Leon, Lou & Morris, Mark & Nikki Calloway, Barbara McKlousky & family, Mr. & Mrs. Melvin Brown & family, Brian "aka Nip", PR, The Stevenson family, Mr. & Mrs. Don Stevenson & family, Ryan & Marcus (Barbers Inc.), Mr. & Mrs. Robert Sheppard, Uncle Hank, Charlie Packard & family, Tom DiFrancesco, Kristy Bilski, & Fulton Books.

My Peace Church Family, Felisha Brown, Mrs. Renee, Robert, AP, Cindy, Mrs. Sheny, Big Dave, Sherri, Pascale, Nate, Belinda, Donna, Jerod, Jordan, Culenthia Preyer, Mrs. Mary & Brandi, Marvin & Vikki, Lou & Morris, Mr. & Mrs. Mike Bailey, Lisa, Pam, & Rodney, Lyn, Officer Crawford & Gulbin.

CHAPTER 1

It All Started Here

Rockford, Illinois, a small industrial town in the Midwest. The population of Rockford in the early eighties was roughly 147,000 people. The city is very friendly and very diverse. People actually spoke to each other despite their color or creed. This was very inviting. The weather in Rockford was very comfortable in the spring and summer months. In the spring, the temperatures would peak to about sixty-five to seventy degrees. In the summer months, the temperature would peak to about eighty to ninety degrees. The winters were just the opposite; they were harsh. At times, the high would be fifteen degrees, and the low would be around two degrees with snow and ice on the ground. The wind chill would take the temperatures even lower, sometimes down to zero.

In 1979, there was a blizzard that was so severe, the temperature plummeted down to negative twenty degrees. The officials declared these conditions to be unsafe and dangerous. They cancelled school for several days, and the citizens had to remain indoors until the temperature rose to a safe level. When looking outside, the snowbanks appeared to be about five feet high. During these times when the weather was this bad, the schools were closed. This would obviously shorten the school days, and the students would have to make this time up at the end of the school year. This was a bittersweet moment for the children. The way they saw it, it was an opportunity to enjoy indoor activities, realizing that at the end of the year the days have to be made up, which slightly extended the school year by several days. Other than that the winter months were not so bad. Making snowmen, snow angels, and ice cream from the snow was a wonderful thing. It was a known fact that if you wanted to make some extra pocket change, then shoveling snow was the way to go.

Enough of the winter season. The fun really came in the spring and summer season. At these times, the citizens had the privilege of visiting several parks including Barber Park, Leven's Lake Park, and Kilbuck Park. These parks were unique in their own way. Many of the students who were in high school were gravitated toward Barber Park. This is where the football and basketball teams would hang out. This is where somebody who is anybody would be on the weekend. (West High versus Auburn High was played at Westburn Stadium, which was the toughest and most-sought-after game of the season.) Barber Park was the best place in the city to find a good pickup game of basketball and flag football. The football players played it safe because if the coaches found out that they were playing full contact, there would be an issue, and there would be repercussions.

Leven's Lake Park is a park where they would fire up the grill, which was conveniently located under the pavilion. A wonderful view of the lake in the background, green grass, and the wind blowing on the trees was definitely a place that one would enjoy and appreciate. On occasion they would have a DJ playing a variety of old-school music. This is also where you would show off your cars as you drove through, waving and shouting at other people that you recognized from school or otherwise; it was like you were in some sort of parade.

Kilbuck Park was more rural. This is where you could walk the trail and enjoy all of what nature had to offer—the trees, the squirrels, the birds, the fresh air, etc. If you just needed to get away from the stresses of life, children, paying bills, society, crime, and your spouse, this is a good place to go. Keeping that balance is very vital. There were events as well as activities for the young teens to indulge in. Let's see, shopping at Symbols. They had the latest fashions in clothes' design and shoes.

There was the Coronado Theater if you wanted to catch up on the latest at the box office. If you wanted to grab some ice cream cones, shaved ice (granita), cotton candy, hot dogs, etc., you could go to Joe's Dairy-ette or Zammuto's restaurants. Box's BBQ is where you would go to get the best barbeque in the Great Midwest. Let's see, you had the east side where teens could hang out at Celebration Station to play the latest arcade games or go to the drive-in movies. If you enjoy roller skating, whether you were a skater or observer, ING Skating Rink was the place to be on Friday, Saturday, or Sunday. There would be a variety of clubs competing for bragging rights as they would display choreography on skates, with every group having their own unique and creative skating styles and outfits to match. They were good too!

To get the best polish sausage with grilled onions and hot peppers, everyone young or old went to Pork Chop Alley located downtown. They should have won some type of national award in some sort of way. The middle schoolers had what they called rec night. This is where the school staff would host a number of activities in which the students would participate in. This would give the boys and girls the chance to reveal themselves for the first time to others, their so-called secret admirers. Can you believe they would shut down the school for that evening on Fridays for several hours so the students could take advantage of the opportunities that were available when their parents were not there? What a blessing, they thought. The dance competitions were a sight to see. Dance groups would compete for bragging rights, city wide. Groups like: "High Voltage", "Master Jam" & "The Rappers Gang"… to name a few, would battle it out.

Now… when it came to seeing your favorite person or group performing onstage, then you would purchase your tickets early. Upon arrival, you would have on your members-only jacket, your penny loafers as casual shoes, your shag hairdo, your Lacoste polo shirt, your Sasson, Jordache, or Vanderbilt jeans and your Old Spice cologne. You were ready for the time of your life when you attended the concerts at Rockford's own MetroCentre arena. There were numerous things that you could do, shop or eat. Rockford was a thriving little city.

CHAPTER 2

The Characters

There are three gentlemen. Bobby, twenty-five, white, and the oldest of the three. He loved to play big brother to the other two. Bobby is 6'1" with red hair, a low-cut bald fade, light mustache, and no other facial hair. He has several tattoos with the locations and the dates of the places that he served at while in the army so that he could not forget the times he had served. Also, to let others know that he served as well. He had a few hobbies—playing poker, fishing, traveling, and shooting at the gun range. Bobby was a loner. He did the majority of things by himself, very independent and self-sufficient. He was raised by his grandmother and grandfather.

It was unfortunate that he lost his parents in his earlier years. They died in a plane crash while vacationing in the Bahamas. His parents sent him some postcards while they were on the island and pictures of them indulging in what they said was paradise. They were waited on hand and foot, spoiled, to say the least. They participated in some trivial game activities that the locals had played host to. They went parasailing, sightseeing, snorkeling, dancing, did boat ride excursions, and gambled. They truly enjoyed themselves. They even said that they had plans for them all to return to the Bahamas with him tagging along. His parents were hardworking people and hadn't taken a vacation in about three years because of the long hours they worked. They agreed that it was time to let their hair down and let people cater to them and not the other way around. His parents stayed on the island for seven days.

About 10:00 am, they boarded the plane on their way back to the States. At about 11:10 am, they were flying about 23,000 feet and climbing to about 32,000 feet before they leveled off. All was well. The issue started when they were descending and approaching the airstrip at about 2,000 feet with speed of about 350 mph. Well, there was a sudden headwind that lifted the plane about 200 feet. The pilot could not regain control of the plane and it slammed to the ground and burned. The plane was small; it carried about forty passengers. It was one of those charter planes that went from the islands to the mainland. There were only twelve survivors, and Bobby's parents were not among them.

Bobby's grandparents raised him. They were strict on him because they wanted the best for him and to shape and mold him to turn out to be a well-disciplined person with respect and morals. They wanted him to apply these things to his life and accomplish all he set out to do. Sometimes Bobby would rebel against his grandparents because he wouldn't always understand the reasons why they were so strict on him, especially early on. Bobby would act out in public sometimes. His grandparents understood why Bobby would misbehave in some cases because they understood that his parents' absence caused him to lash out.

Again Bobby, was a loner and usually kept to himself. With no siblings, he did not develop many social skills early on. In his early twenties, he had an abundance of testosterone and energy and would blew off steam every now and then. He decided to pursue his career in the army. He was stationed in California at a well-known army base. This was a major life changer for him. Not only because of the environment but the climate as well. Eventually, he realized that he had to deal with his superiors, just as he dealt with his grandparents when he was younger.

Next is Tony, who is twenty-five and black. He is seven months younger than Bobby. Most of the time he would remind Bobby how only a few months separated them. He let him know in not so many words that he was not that much older than him. He was also taller than Bobby. He stood at 6'3", had a scar on the left side of his chin; had a bald head, and a few tattoos of his own. But his tattoos were on his arms and legs, displaying the names of his siblings and his nickname or alias.

Tony had a more outgoing personality. He was not shy in any form of the word. He could strike up a conversation with a complete stranger, whether it be at the mall, the car wash, the park, the grocery store, etc. His upbringing was different from the other two. He was brought up in a two-parent household with two other siblings. Tony did the best he could in just about everything he attempted. He was the second of three children, and both of his parents were involved in their upbringing. They didn't sugarcoat anything when it came to the challenges of life as minorities.

Joey is twenty-four, white. He is close to 6'2", slender, weighing about 185 pounds. He too had tattoos on his person. He wore the navy anchor on his forearm and a larger anchor of the same kind on his calf muscle, except this one had his initials below the anchor and the American flag on top of the anchor. He had a light fade as well, military cut, like Bobby. He had no facial hair and had a goatee with several cuts and bruises on his arms. Both of his parents were still living as well. He also had two younger brothers and a girlfriend. Joey enlisted and served in the navy on a well-known aircraft carrier specializing in clerical communications. After high school he got into trouble.

Before I explain, I would like to give you a little background on Joey. Joey was brought up in a well-established home. His parents would take him to church along with his younger brothers. They were actually involved in their children's lives. While in elementary, middle, and high school, Joey was involved in sports from soccer to baseball and football throughout the years, and not necessarily in that order. He was pretty good at soccer and football, but not so much in baseball. His parents did not dare tell him this. This would have damaged his ambitions and motivations in life. They understood how important that would be for him and his siblings. They encouraged him nonetheless. They not only paid for his registration fees and equipment. They would also attend every game that he played in and cheered him on. They would attend PTA meetings, award presentations, school events, field trips, charity events (such as selling baked goods and paraphernalia, for example, wind chimes, paper weights, candles, ornaments, stationery, etc. From an order form). Joey's grades weren't bad at all, averaging about a B for the year. The older he got, the lower the grades. He had other influences like girls, video games, and marijuana. This concludes the characters' introductions.

CHAPTER 3

Elementary and Middle School

On the playground at West View Elementary School, three young boys meet on the asphalt playing kickball. Kickball was sort of like baseball. There was a big round red ball. The pitcher would roll the ball to the kicker who was up, and the kicker would kick the ball hopefully in an area where no one was; so that he could advance to as many bases as possible before the opposite team would throw the ball at him attempting to put him out. The ball had to hit him to be declared out. But if the kicker kicked the ball in the air and someone caught it, then this would also be declared an out; and you had to get three outs before the other team would go up to kick; and so forth. It was the third grade, and the boys averaged about ten years of age.

The boys would select the teams that would compete with one another. They would flip a coin to select two captains. These were the two people with the highest GPA in the six-week term of the school. This had to be proven by bringing their report cards to the playground before the teams were selected. The captains would then try and recruit the top players that were lined up along the fence. The elected captains would go back and forth with their player selections until there was no one left. Of course, they would try and select the best players possible early on so that they could claim the victory and bragging rights, until the next meeting. Then this process would start all over again.

Of all the kids that participated in the games, three of the boys spent more time together than the others. The things that they did and the things that they talked about were, for the most part, in agreement, and none of what they talked about involved girls. That came later on. The boys' were Joey, Bobby and Tony; they were inseparable. If you saw one of them, the others would not be far behind. All three boys were pretty smart. They all got good grades. Sometimes, when there were problems one could not solve, they would help one another whether it be math, english, history, or science. The friendship that they had was unusual, the teachers had noticed this as well. It was uncommon. There would be times when the boys would have disagreements among themselves when it came time for them to make group decisions about something. They would either iron them out with reason, or depending on the day, it would get physical.

However, if and when there was a conflict with an "outsider," as they called them, they understood that the rules would change at that point. If someone came into their circle and violated anyone of them, it was game on, no matter the circumstances. Loyalty is what they believed in.

Sometimes, the boys would spend the night at one another's. There would be times when Joey's mother would pick him up from school, arriving at 3:00 pm. Occasionally, the other boys would join them. They normally caught the bus, which would leave at 3:15 pm, and the ride would take them an extra fifteen minutes. So the time lapsed would be thirty minutes before they would make it home from the time the last school bell had rung. So catching a ride with Joey is a good thing.

On Fridays, Joey's mom would sometimes ask Bobby and Tony if they wanted to stay the night, if their moms would approve. So she would call their moms on her cell phone and ask. Their moms had actually known each other. Most of the time, they would approve, unless there was a special family function going on such as vacationing or holidays. Other than that, the moms, for the most part, would almost always allow the boys to sleep over, so they can have some time to themselves, whether it be shopping or just nothing but sitting around the house.

Tony and Bobby did not stay far from Joey, so his mom would take them home to grab an overnight bag, and to Joey's house they went. When they got there, the boys, being boys, took their bags and threw them down right where they stood. It was as though it was the official sign that the weekend had just begun. They all went to Joey's room. Each one proceeded to look for their favorite video game. It didn't take them long to do. They took turns playing, two at a time. The only time they took a break was when Joey's mother called them to eat or when they went to the bathroom. As the night progressed, the boys had to keep quiet because they would normally stay up later than Joey's parents. Saturdays mornings were the best. They would sleep late and wake up with absolutely no chore to do. They absolutely loved this. They had it all figured out. Not home, no chores; this was their slogan and knew that there was nothing expected of them while they were at Joey's.

Every now and then, Joey's father would ask the boys if they wanted to make some extra money by helping him in the garage with some projects that he worked on. He was very crafty, and all the boys, at some time or another, had learned something.

For the most part, the boys would just sit around the television with a big bowl of cereal and watch their favorite cartoons for the rest of the morning, if Joey's mother hadn't prepared breakfast for them.

Now in their teens, the boys had physically grown up. Their bodies were changing; puberty is what they call this. Their voices turned bass, and they had girls on their minds, and so forth. Because they stayed so close together, the teens were in the same school district, and they attended the same middle school as well. Remember, it was a small town.

There were a few privileges that came with being a teen. The times that they had to be at home on school nights were extended. They had a little more freedom. They were trusted more by their parents. They did not have to call in as often. Life was great!

On a good day, the teens would go down to the nearby creek, find small rocks, preferably the long flat ones so they could skip them across the surface of the water, competing with one another to see who created the most ripples in the water. The reward that the teens would get was bragging rights. If the weather permitted, they would get their fishing poles, get some live bait, and go fishing.

The teens were responsible. They saved the money that they made helping Joey's father do different projects and repairs around the house. Yes, even in their teens, Joey's father still provided them with tasks, so they could have a little pocket change. He would allow them to work as long as they wanted to on the weekends. The more they worked, the more they earned. The teens made a decent amount of money for their ages.

They also bought skateboards, and each one of the skateboards represented their personalities. Bobby liked the color blue so he took off the factory-made wheels and replaced them with wider custom-made blue wheels that he ordered in a catalog. He peeled off the factory paper on the surface of the board and creatively made a sandpaper abrasion surface. He did this by buying sandpaper, spray paint, and some adhesive at the hardware store.

Joey's color was red, and he did the same, and Tony's was green, and he also did the same. The teens learned to identify and use certain hand tools by helping Joey's dad on the weekends. Small projects were the very things that the teens lived for. Times when they were adventurous, they would go to abandoned warehouses and collect a few things that they considered treasures and took them home. Of course, we would consider this junk. It was rare to find the teens sitting around doing nothing.

Joey, Bobby, and Tony would often spend time visiting each other's homes; still helping one another with their homework. There were times when the teens would rotate and eat at each other's homes. They all experienced different types of food as they went from house to house. The most interesting moment was when Joey and Bobby ate at Tony's house for the first time. This is when they experienced collard greens and hot water cornbread. This was one of the few unique dishes that were served at Tony's parents' home. "Soul food" is what they called it. Joey and Bobby both loved it. Don't get me wrong, Tony had his fair share of chicken fried steak, and mashed potatoes, to say the least, and he loved it! These young teens did everything together. Again, they were inseparable.

Recreation night at Roosevelt Middle School is something that the seventh and eighth graders looked forward to. This is the time that teachers and staff would host a night for all the students to hang out on Friday night and mingle with other students. The entire school would be shut down that Friday evening only for this event to take place. Rec night started at 7:00 pm and went on until 11:00 pm. They had many activities and things to do such as playing basketball, dancing with a live DJ, swimming, drawings for prizes, movies and table games such as; Ping-Pong, foosball, billiards, and a few more games. This was also an opportunity to sneak in a kiss or a hug with the one you truly had a crush on. There were dark corners that you could hide in, for this to take place. There were no parents there and with there being such a small staff they had many opportunities to accomplish this.

The young teens set their sights and ambitions in another direction. They were responsible, a little reckless, but responsible. All three teens worked in the afternoon program at Booker T. Washington Center. The program only lasted for nine weeks during the summer vacation. They made about sixty dollars a week while in the program. Not bad, after all, this was the eighties. So with the money they made on the weekends helping Joey's father and being in the summer program, they were able to go to the mall on the weekends and splurge, enabling them to buy the latest video games. Essentially, the teens would get paid to learn. They would learn things about computers, monitors, and modems when they were first introduced, so they were able to grasp the knowledge of technology early on.

On this particular day, Tony and Joey went over to Bobby's to pay him a visit. When they arrived, there were a couple of police cars outside of his house. This was odd. They paused for a moment, looked at each other with concern, and proceeded up the sidewalk to the house. The teens knocked on the door, and to their surprise, Bobby's grandparents answered. They didn't look so good. The grandparents gestured the two of them to come inside. Once they closed the door, the teens asked what was going on and where Bobby was. They responded that he was in his room and didn't want any company. They asked them to sit down. So they explained to them that Bobby's parents were killed in a plane accident. His grandparents were filled with emotion, they turned away and began to cry.

Tony and Joey were just like mannequins. They sat there for a few seconds and also began to cry. Once everyone got their composure back, the grandparents went on to say that this was why Bobby was in his room. The guys slowly got up from their seats and slowly walked to the front door with their hands wiping away their tears. At the same time, one of them said, "We understand," and told them that they would call to check up on them.

A few days later, Bobby called Tony and told him that he was feeling pretty bad and did not know how to face them. At that time, Tony made a suggestion to Bobby to meet him and Joey at the park. So Tony called Joey and let him know what he and Bobby talked about; he thought this would be a good idea. The whole reasoning behind it was that they wanted to comfort Bobby.

The teens all met at the park in the afternoon. When they saw Bobby, his eyes were cherry red… understandably so. Once they were there, Joey was the first to speak. He told Bobby that what he was feeling was what they were feeling also. They told him that it was going to take time to heal, and that they were always there for him. Tony put his hand on Bobby's shoulder and says if he felt like hanging out to take his mind off of things for a while; it might be helpful to go over to Tony's and play some video games.

Earlier that day, Tony had mentioned to his mom what had happened, so his mom called Bobby's home and gave her condolences asking them to call if they needed anything. In the meantime, she told Tony that she would prepare Bobby's favorite soul food dish. When Tony told Bobby of this, it put a temporary smile on his face. This was the beginning of healing for Bobby.

As time went on, Tony or Joey would not speak of Bobby's parents unless he initiated it. Again, these young teens were one of a kind. There was nothing they wouldn't do for one another.

CHAPTER 4

The Summer

A few years have passed since the misfortune of Bobby's parents. Bobby stays with his grandparents who also stayed in the same neighborhood. He would always think about his parents and realized that the thought would never go away. He used their absence to encourage and motivate him. However, if his grandmother asked him to finish a chore, he would say harsh things to her or would ignore her altogether. Sometimes his grandfather would treat them out for pizza or ice cream on Fridays to keep the family together socially. Bobby would have tantrums if his order was not correct. If he was asked to do something as simple as hold the door open for someone that is handicapped, he would not only hold the door open; he would also make a sarcastic statement or gesture. He would not always get his way. Sometimes, his grandfather would have to chastise him.

While in high school, Bobby found a part-time job working at McDonald's. He started working in the lobby emptying the trash receptacles, wiping down the tables, and cleaning the restrooms. For about seven months, this would be his assignment. Bobby thought it would be a blast to work the grill, so he talked to the manager and asked her what the likelihood would be of becoming a grill master. The manager liked the idea that he wanted to move up and told him that he would have to learn how to work the other stations; such as the ovens, and fryers. The manager showed him where to find the items he would need and also where to find various food items he would be preparing. He was excited about the wonderful opportunity that the manager had allowed him. He gladly accepted the role because he could not advance with just cleaning alone.

Like all jobs of interest, you would have to be trained first. He struggled some, but the manager saw the potential in him and did not give up on him. The manager had a coworker by the name of Markus who knew his way around the grill. He showed Bobby his skills and was assigned to train Bobby. Markus worked at McDonald's for about three years and knew how to work all stations, and he was good at what he did. Markus also got along with people, which made the transition much smoother. Working on the grill took dedication. You have to like what you do. Bobby picked up on this faster than he thought. He started off grilling one to two dozen burgers at one time and worked his way up to three. Quite an accomplishment, he was told.

Grilling was not the cleanest job that there was. It paid a little more, but it was not the cleanest. After his shift was over, he would call a family member to check and see if they were available to pick him up. His grandfather taught him how to drive; he did have his driver's license, but he did not own a car. His grandparents would allow him to borrow the car on the weekends, but during the weekdays, they had errands to run and doctor's appointments to keep. So rather than him having the car at work and just sitting there, they were able to use the vehicle. Sometimes he was fortunate to get a ride home, and other times he was not.

Bobby lived about six miles from the restaurant, so he would have no choice but to walk home sometimes. He would have to walk to work also; if his grandparents needed the car when he was scheduled to work. Their times would sometimes conflict. Bobby endured the circumstances. He knew it would not be long before he purchased his own vehicle. He was saving his money. The front of his uniform was covered with grease and saturated areas that the apron had not covered, it was pretty bad. The times that he walked home, he noticed that the dogs would bark as he walked by. He caught their attention because he smelled like an oversized Big Mac. When he finally got home, he would wash his uniform with soap. Of course this got rid of the smell, but not the stains.

Tony played football at the local high school with the Warriors. He played the position of wide receiver. He had to pay for most of his football equipment. His parents did what they could to help with most of the cost. They had two other children to care for, so ultimately, he had to pay the difference of what his parents gave him; if he wanted to play. He would do odd jobs like shine shoes, paint, and mow yards. Tony would spend most of the summer doing these odd jobs; preparing for football in the upcoming fall season. His summers were short-lived for the most part. There were times when he would hang out on the weekends to bring balance in his life.

Joey was unemployed at the time. Occasionally, the three would go to one of the popular hangouts and play arcade games. They would place wagers with one another to see who would get the high score for that night. They would also play eight ball and make bets of whoever won the best of ten games. Other times, they would hang out at the drive-in theater. In order to save money, they would take two vehicles. The theater would only charge you per vehicle, no matter how many persons were inside. They weren't really concerned about comfort. The teenagers took advantage of this on the weekends.

Tony and Bobby had girlfriends. Joey had mentioned to Tony on a couple of occasions that he wanted to meet a special girl, so Tony called his girlfriend Cheryl and asked her if she knew anyone that was not dating at that time. Yvette immediately popped into Cheryl's head. Although Cheryl and Yvette went to two different high schools, they were the best of friends. She called Tony and left him a message on his voice mail, asking him if he had any plans for the upcoming weekend. Once he received the message, he called her back. She told him that Yvette did not have a boyfriend at the time and was willing to meet Joey. Based on what Cheryl had told her about his personality and appearance, she was willing to meet him.

Cheryl put the plan in motion, setting up the date on Saturday at the drive-in theater. It was close to 8:00 pm. Tony and Cheryl were in Cheryl's car. They picked up Yvette from her home, along the way. Once they got there, Yvette bombarded them with a lot of questions, as they headed over to pick up Joey. She didn't normally do blind dates, but she made an exception this time.

They arrived at Joey's. He was standing on the curb when they pulled up. This is when they make eye contact for the first time. They all got out of the car, Tony and Joey bumped fists and hugged one another, the new way of greeting your fellow brother. He then hugged Cheryl and went over to Yvette. He formally introduced himself by reaching out his hand showing some courtesy as he said to her, "Pleased to meet you, Yvette."

With a smile on her face, she also extended her hand and met him halfway. She said with pleasure, "Pleased to meet you as well, Joey."

Everyone then got into the car, and off they went to the movie theater. While they were on their way to the drive-in, they all were engaged in conversation and laughter. The conversation was mostly about school. By this time, it was about 8:45 pm and was almost completely dark. As they approached the entrance to the drive-in, Joey looked ahead for the best spot to set up, he made a gesture to Tony while asking, "What do you all think about that spot?"

As I stated earlier, you only get charged per vehicle when at the drive-in theater, which is why everyone was picked up. Once they got settled down, Joey was the first to break the ice. He engaged Yvette in small talk. He then offered, as a gentleman would, to buy her any snack she wanted.

Yvette smiled at him again as she accepted his offer, "You are sweet and considerate."

Joey then gestures Tony to go with him to get some snacks and Tony says to him, "I was headed that way myself, let's go."

While they were in line, Joey said to Tony, "I like her as a person, and damn, she's good lookin'!"

As the night went on, Joey, still being considerate, asked Yvette if he could put his arm around her and he didn't want to be too aggressive. He thought that she was attractive and wanted to relish his thoughts and make them a reality. She gladly accepted for the second time.

Cheryl looked over her shoulder and made a comment to Joey, "She must like you because this is not something that Yvette would allow if she didn't take a liking to someone."

"It was a good thing" she said as she turned back around and kissed Tony. Joey and Yvette exchanged phone numbers as the evening came to an end.

They both kept in constant contact with one another. Joey found out that Yvette ran track for the high school that she attended. Her event was the long jump. She had track practice five to six days a week. Because of this they hadn't talked much. Three weeks later, track season started, and she invited him to the track meet. He watched her perform at the invitational. The first attempts that she made were not her personal best, and you could see that she was frustrated. So when it was not yet her turn to jump, Joey gestured her over to him and made a joke. He stated that if she would get her mind off him and focus, then maybe she would be satisfied with the attempts she would make from that point forward. He gave her a peck on the cheek and stated that he believed in her. This encouraged her to do better.

The following week, they both made plans that weekend to hang out at the video arcade to avoid the stresses of life for a moment. Yvette and Joey saw each other often enough to consider themselves officially boyfriend and girlfriend. When track season was over, Yvette had more time to spare. So after she finished her homework, she immediately called Joey. He had time to spend with his sweetheart as long as he didn't have a lot of homework, or didn't have to work. They both hung around each other's families.

Yvette spent time with Joey's younger brothers. She was a positive influence to them both. She would sometimes take them to the park or go out for ice cream or play video games with them. If the youngsters knew she was coming over, they would literally wait for her at the front door, peeking out the window every thirty seconds until she arrived.

Joey's uncle had a cookout, and Joey asked his uncle if he could invite a couple of Yvette's relatives over to enjoy some of his good cooking. Joey's uncle told him that it was OK; but that they may want to bring their own drinks in case he did not have what they liked to drink. Other than that, he was OK with them coming over.

Yvette brought her brother and aunt along. The cookout was on Saturday around 2:00 pm. Joey's uncle was known for throwing parties and was also known for his good cooking. Yvette and her two family members arrived at about 2:30 pm. With his apron on, Joey's uncle introduced himself and invited them inside. The first thing that Yvette's aunt asked him was, "Do you need help with anything? I know my way around the kitchen as well."

He told her that he wanted them to relax, grab a drink, and listen to the music that he was playing; unless they wanted to hear something different. Other than that, he had things in the kitchen in check. He was very polite. Joey's uncle seemed to enjoy Yvette's aunt because he continually asked her if she was enjoying herself more than usual, and it was noticed by everyone. He even asked her to join him on the dance floor when one of his favorite oldies was playing, she gladly accepted. Oh, what fun it was!

As the evening progressed, the fun continued. They all decided to play a board game. Of course, Joey's uncle chose Yvette's aunt to be his partner. After the games were over they all parted ways. His uncle and her aunt had an extensive conversation; they also exchanged phone numbers. They all talk about this cookout till this day.

Joey called Yvette one particular day, asking her if she wanted to do a daring thing. Her being curious she asked him, "What are you up to?"

Joey responded, "Listen, how would you like to play hooky and just spend time with each other, if you know what I mean?"

She responded by asking him when and where. Joey replied that he had it all figured out. He asked her what time her mother left for work, and she responded about 8:00 am; but she would leave the house as early as 7:30 am. He then said, "That's perfect."

So she, playing stupid, and asked him why this was important, and he replied, "I want us to have a little fun."

Yvette had a grin on her face and said, "I'm game! How do we do this?"

Joey said, "This is what we can do. This coming Tuesday, we both will go to school and attend our first class. Then we will claim that we are sick with stomachaches which the nurses couldn't prove as long as we play the role. They would eventually send us home." (Remember, they attended different high schools). "I will catch the bus, and you can pick me up on the corner of Washington and Cedar Boulevard."

This was three blocks from Yvette's house. They would meet up about 9:30 am, and that way, they would have a decent amount of time to spend together, before her mom got home.

She replied, "Wow! If you were a bank robber, I'm almost certain you would have pulled it off." Joey burst out with laughter. So they both executed the plan and it all worked out. They were intimate for the next few hours.

There were about five weeks left in the summer, and the weather began to change. Joey called Bobby and Tony. He told them that his dad had some extra tickets to the air show in Springfield he wanted Joey to call them and see if they would be interested in going. Joey and his dad went every year. Before Joey called them back, he called Yvette and told her about the trip that he and his dad took every year, and it was about that time and he would be leaving for the weekend. Again, Joey and Yvette made plans to meet up on Thursday to have lunch together.

Once he asked Bobby and Tony if they wanted to go, they were filled with excitement. Joey said his dad would fill them in on the details once they got the approval from their parents (grandparents in Bobby's case). Bobby called up his grandparents and told them that he would like to speak with them when he got home. Once he got home, both of his grandparents were there, and he asked if it would be OK if he attended the air show with Joey and his dad. He also mentioned that Tony may be tagging along as well. All his grandparents wanted for him was to enjoy his life and to be with the people that he was friends with and the ones they felt comfortable with. They also realized that this would be good therapy for Bobby, so they did not hesitate to approve of the trip. After he thanked them, he told his grandparents that Joey's dad would give them all the details, and he would then pass the information to them.

Tony also called ahead telling his mother that he wanted to talk to her and his dad when he got home. Moments later, when Tony got home and shared the news of the trip, his dad was OK with it, but his mom, on the other hand, was not so sure. She said Springfield was a long way away, and this was the first time Tony had been this far from home. (For a mom, going thirty miles from home was a big thing in her mind.) His mom then asked him to call Joey and ask if his father could come over and share the details with her. Tony was embarrassed, but he did honor her wishes. So Joey's dad agreed to meet up with her the next day.

At this time, Tony called Cheryl and told her what was going on and how his mom was freaking out. Cheryl found this to be quite amusing. She wanted to stop by his house to give him a hug and kiss to see him off. Joey's dad arrived the following day. Tony's mom had some specific questions for him: how long it would take, where they would stay, what he would eat, and so on. Tony's dad politely interrupted her and said, "Let the boy go to the air show. It's not like he's going to China. Besides, he needs to get away. He needs balance after working long hours and football practice."

After he put things into perspective, her mind was at ease.

Joey's father supplied her with all the information she needed. It was now Tuesday, and the air show was on the upcoming Saturday, at noon. This was perfect for Tony. He had no football practice on Fridays, which allowed him to go. Joey was unemployed which allowed him to go and Bobby asked someone to fill in for him from Friday to Monday at McDonald's which allowed him to go. His manager gave him the approval now that he had someone to cover his shift. Bobby then informed his grandparents of all the information about the trip.

Joey's dad picked up the boys at Tony's house about 2:00 pm. With duffel bags thrown over their shoulders, they were ready to go. They made a stop to gas up and grab a bite to eat. It was about 3:30 pm when they were actually on the interstate headed for Springfield, The Land of Lincoln. Off they went. The trip would take about three hours. While they were in the car, Joey's dad wanted to excite them even more by explaining to them what it was that they were actually going to see. He described some of the war planes that would be at the show and what their purpose was. They were so excited that they all turned red, including Tony! Joey's dad was extremely knowledgeable about the air show and the planes. He was once in the military as a plane mechanic. The weekend was indescribable. The three young men continued to bond. It was amazing how close of a bond these three young men had. Inseparable!

CHAPTER 5

Fall Season

School started at the end of August. Cheryl, Bobby, Tony, and Yvette were all seniors, and Joey was a junior. They were excited to begin the school year because they would be graduating in the summer the following year, except Joey.

Cheryl, Joey, Yvette, and Bobby all went to the big game between Auburn High and West High to see Tony play in the most anticipated game in the city of Rockford. The game was so popular that all the high schools in the district showed up to witness the best game of the season. Despite their win or loss record for the season both teams continue to make the play-offs in consecutive years; more than any other school in the district. This game was played once a year. The stadium was filled to capacity. As always, at the beginning of all games, the National Atheneum was sung first, then the announcer would introduce the visiting team first and the home team second. Afterward, they would announce the starters of both teams. In this case, the Auburn Knights were the visiting team, and the West Warriors were the home team.

When they introduced the West Warrior starters the crowd went wild. Tony was next to be announced. His supporting staff had cheered until their voices became hoarse, especially Cheryl's voice. "Standing at 6'3" and weighing 210 pounds, playing wide receiver for the Warriors wearing number 27."

Tony practiced five or sometimes six days a week; it paid off for him. He was one of the top receivers on his team. His performance last season showed that his stats were incredible, with 95 completions for 1,020 yards for the year, including playoffs.

The game was hard-hitting. How hard? At halftime, when the big linemen would head to the locker room; if you were close to the field, you could see blood on the jerseys of the players on both sides. The game was close. At the final whistle, Auburn had beaten West High by 5 points, but despite it all, Tony had a good game, pulling down 15 catches for 155 yards.

While on the field, he had his head down with his helmet in his left hand. He went over to Cheryl and the rest of the crew. She hugged him while telling him that she loved him and the others gave him a hug and a high five. After the game, both teams headed for the showers. Once Tony and the other players got dressed into their street clothes, it was a common thing for them to meet back at the school that night attempting to boost morale; looking forward to the next game or next season, whichever the case. This was a ritual that was carried on from school year to school year.

There were always activities that the school would host for the seniors. They were also privileged as well. One of the privileges is that the students would have extended lunch periods.

Other privileges were hanging out at the student union hall, playing dominoes and cards. They were pretty much spoiled.

One more event that was scheduled for the seniors was movie night at the local movie theater. The seniors would purchase tickets that went on sale starting Monday and could purchase tickets for the duration of that week. The theater would show one of the latest blockbuster hits on Fridays of the same week. This was offered exclusively to the seniors once a year.

The last of the events, was an upcoming senior dance that was scheduled in the month of November. The students had to purchase the tickets early to attend. The three of them were pretty much involved in mostly anything the school had to offer, especially in their senior year.

Basketball season had recently started, and the Warriors were ranked #4 in the state. They were scheduled to play against Boylan High School, which was ranked #2 in the state. Both teams were to play tomorrow night at the 40,000-seat MetroCentre in downtown Rockford for the district title. Whoever won would advance to the state championship, that would be played at the state capital.

So with that being said, the trio purchased tickets to attend the most anticipated event that was to take place that weekend. Joey and Yvette, along with Tony and Cheryl, and Bobby all attended. Bobby was accompanied by Jackie, a girl he recently met at the dance that the school hosted previously. Just like the students did for the football season, they did the same for basketball season. They had a pep rally. This rally was inspired by a gentleman named Brian. Every student body, from the freshmen to the seniors, had a representative for that class.

Brian was undoubtedly the chosen one for the senior class. Brian was school spirited. He would be the one to single-handedly encourage the seniors and the other classes as well. After all, the other classes would imitate the senior class. He had a character like no other. He was no doubt one of the smartest guys at school. If the basketball team struggled with their grades, he would assist them and keep them eligible to participate in the games that they were scheduled to play. Not that the players were incompetent, they practiced daily and had little time for studying, especially if they made the playoffs. The players would go to him, and he would tutor them either on a one on one or as a group, depending on the subject matter. Brian knew the players well enough that when a player was interviewed by the local newspaper at the end of the game because of his stats; he would acknowledge Brian and give him a shout-out. Or if it were multiple players, they would do the same.

He was the one who was responsible for the events that the senior class participated in. The school itself hadn't scheduled many off campus events for the seniors. He had encouraged the school staff to let the senior class have a bonfire of their own. He was also involved in any fund-raising to help the players get new uniforms or just extra money for the teams' traveling expenses. He also came up with the idea to have a car wash for the students in the spring months so that the senior class would have extra money for prom in the upcoming months.

Not only did the car washes give them extra spending change, it was an opportunity for the young men to witness the young ladies in their swimsuits. Because of this, the young men would miss a spot or two, if you know what I mean.

Brian met Bobby and Joey through Tony. Everyone knows that if you see Tony, then naturally, Bobby and Joey would not be far behind. One day, Brian got together with Bobby and Tony. While at the student union hall, he asked them what they thought about having a snowball fight with the males and females of the senior class. He told them that since he had favor with the school staff, he could use his wits and persuade the school staff members to let the senior class have a ditch day. He asked them to keep this idea a secret because if it leaked out and another student tried to do this, it would be a bust because others didn't have the influence to carry out the brilliant task.

So the trio didn't say a word to anyone, not even their significant others, until they got the approval from Brian himself. Once Brian was in the office, he asked if the principal was available. One of the office staff members went to the principal's door, which was open, and asked the principal if he had a minute to visit with Brian. The principal who knew him well invited him in his office. He starts off by saying, thanks for allowing him the time to visit. Brian was avid. He proceeded by saying that the senior class would not be around this time next year and that he wanted the class to maximize the moment, of these last school days.

The principal then asked, "What are you proposing? And knowing you, I'm sure that it's going to be interesting."

This is when he mentioned the snowball fight. The principal wanted specific details on the location and the time, so Brian enlightened him on the details. He did not hesitate to give him the approval. This took every bit of fifteen minutes. There was a huge grin on Brian's face as he extended his hand and thanked the principal. Brian knew that if he pulled this off, this would favorably put him in front of the other candidates as he ran for president. Oh, by the way, he was running for president of the senior class, and there was a method to his madness. Not only was he helping his class, he understood that the class would be helping him, by getting potential votes. He had the spirit and loved his school. Again, he was no dummy by far. He summoned Bobby and Tony, letting them know that they could open the floodgates and let all the senior class know of the upcoming event, that was to take place on Thursday; two days from then. Tony and Bobby would often tease Joey because he was not a senior and could not participate in the snowball fight. Joey didn't take kindly to this. He did not hesitate to let them know in so many words.

The day had come. The snowball fight was in full effect. Bobby, and Tony, along with their mates and the rest of the senior class attended the event. All the students had prepared by putting on extra layers of clothing to protect them from the projectiles that would be imposed on them; they also had extra layers of socks to keep them warm. (This was the norm. If you didn't want to feel the full thrust of a two-pound compact snowball approaching you at 40 mph, you'd be a fool if you didn't have that additional protection.) They played among each another for several hours, coming up with different ways to compete. Starting as boys versus girls didn't work out as planned. The girls were overwhelmed, so they started over and picked teams that involved both genders to mix. This was an opportunity for Bobby and Jackie to get more acquainted. He deliberately threw snowballs in her direction to get her attention. There was about one hour of daylight left before the sun went completely down.

Brian had announced that they were going to Kilbuck Park and light the bonfire. Kilbuck Park was not far from the school, and this would allow them plenty of time to light the fire before it got dark. The class quickly decided to have the majority of the guys head out to the site and get the fire going while most of the girls would eventually show up. They were accompanied by only a few guys who stayed behind for their convenience and safety. One good thing about the senior class was that they always had the wood stacked and ready to burn at a moment's notice. About one to two hours later, the sun was completely down, and so was the temperature at thirty-five degrees Fahrenheit. There was just snow and no ice at that time, so this made conditions tolerable. The bonfire was completely engulfed in flames, its peak reached thirty feet high. It was beautiful, and you could feel the heat from about forty feet away.

At this time, the last of the vehicles had arrived. All the seniors gathered around the fire with their significant others by their side. With the shadow of the flame moving and radiating off the many smiling faces of both the boys and the girls; the temperature really went up! They all were enjoying the ambiance that the fire provided.

Bobby pulled Jackie toward him, and they hugged each other.

Jackie looked into his eyes and said, "So tell me, how did you Tony and Joey meet? And how did you guys grow so close to each other?"

Bobby replied and told her the full story. He went further to say, "We have this bond that is unbreakable and we refuse to let one another down despite the circumstances. We have nothing to prove except to one another. We will be with each other until death do us part, unless something that is out of our control happens, even then, we have loyalty to see it through no matter the cost; and I speak for all of us. If you ask them the same, you will get the exact same response. There may be little mercy on those who attempt to deceive or threaten us."

The entire school was completely aware of the trio and their relationship. They were aware of what the consequences might be if they disrespected any of them. Jackie looked at him to weigh the seriousness of his expression and concluded that he was very sincere in what he was saying. Jackie thought to herself this was extremely rare for someone to feel so strongly about another; and not be related, let alone the cultural differences that they had. The fact that they were males made it even more unique. She asked him why he was so strong-willed, and he told her that he had to be, as he lost his parents at an early age. He felt that no one else was going to take care of him. "Furthermore there was only a small amount of people who give a damn about you, and these are the ones you trust and keep in your circle; other than that, you control your own destiny." What you put in is what you'll get out; Whether it be time, effort, understanding, education, commitment, quality, and quantity, just to name a few.

His intellect and knowledge of life at a young age drew him close to Jackie. Again, she thought that a person with this much drive would make for a good husband one day. It's a type of security and comfort that one needs. Their conversation went a little further. She told him about the trials that she had gone through growing up with an older sister; how there were only two of them and how her dad had given them favor because they were females. He showed them tough love, not in an abusive way, but he prepared them to cope with life. He told and showed them how to survive and not to depend solely on a man, but at the same time be able to recognize a good man if he showed up on the porch. He showed them how to defend themselves and to always be aware of their surroundings. Their father also taught them sense of direction, both literally and figuratively.

It was close to Yvette's birthday. This was a special year for her. It would be the last birthday that she would celebrate as a senior in high school. Joey knew this and, taking this into consideration, he summed a couple of Yvette's closest friends and asked them to help coordinate a surprise birthday party for her. Joey discreetly called others who were mutual friends of hers and got their contact information. Once he received the information, he scheduled a meeting to meet with them. He gave them the time and address where they all would meet up. It was actually the same place that the surprise party would take place.

The place was called Jonathan's Hall, a place that you could rent out by the hour, it was capable of holding about 300 people with three coed restrooms and a full kitchen. The hall also had lots of seating with folding tables and chairs along with table linings and trash receptacles. There was also plenty of parking to accommodate the guests. This was all included in the rental agreement. The agreement was signed by Joey and the property manager for the total cost of $500 for six hours. He had to give a down payment in the amount of $150 to hold the hall for the upcoming day, which was Friday, October 18 (Yvette's birthday). Joey decided to kill two birds with one stone and have the ladies meet him there so they could see how the floor plan looked; he could also make the down payment at the same time, which saved him a trip.

All three of them agreed to meet at the hall about 3:30 pm. Joey arrived at the hall about twenty minutes early and paid the deposit. He then was given full access to the hall. When the two ladies showed up, they walked the property and planned and coordinated all things that would take place. Joey told them that his responsibilities would be to pay for the hall, the food, drinks, and any party favorites—balloons, streamers, DJ, chocolate fountain, party hats, etc. Joey had a friend that was into photography, and this friend owed him a favor. He informed the ladies that he was not good at planning or preparation. This was where they could come in and help. Carol and Jasmine were their names. Carol agreed to be responsible for the buying and preparation of the food. And Jasmine was responsible for setting up and decorating the hall.

Joey had no favors with the DJ. He had to pay him! But the price was right, only $150 for the night, and it was a steal according to Joey. October 3rd is when this all took place, so all parties involved had ample amount of time to plan, pay, and set up the event. Jasmine and Carol both told Joey how good of a person he was to host the event. They further went on to say that this showed just how much he cared for Yvette, and had not mentioned that the cost would be an issue.

Joey replied, "All that you say is true for me to pay almost $1,000 to please my girl. This, I'm willing to do, so thank you."

"This is why we are here," Carol said. "That's our girl, and we will do whatever it takes to make this surprise party a success."

Whether Joey was working or not, he always kept a sufficient amount of money away for safekeeping, and this was how he funded this event. Joey had confidence in the ladies to use their judgment to purchase the items needed, the quantity and quality. They trusted that he would reimburse them if necessary. He could not be with them always, if something were forgotten he asked them to use their better judgment to purchase such items.

There were lots of whispering and secrets being shared at this point. People were trying to be as discreet as possible, attempting to keep Yvette off balance so that she would remain clueless as to what was going on.

The day had arrived. Jasmine did a wonderful job with the decorations. She knew Yvette's favorite colors and took this into consideration when purchasing the items that she needed to beautify the hall. The colors were burgundy and white. When you walked into the hall, everything from the balloons to the table coverings and everything between were covered in these colors. The coordination should have won some type of award if there was any such thing. The hall was absolutely gorgeous.

Carol did not fall short of complementing the decorations with the food that she prepared. Carol had fruits carved in ways that were unique. She served a variety of different dishes. There were also finger foods that were put in place as appetizers for those who couldn't wait. The aroma coming from the kitchen should have also won an award. They both went all in!

The DJ was in place. He showed up about two hours prior and was ready to go. The photographer had arrived early as well to set up a good spot for those who wanted to take individual or coupled shots. The photographer also went around taking group shots as well. It was close to 7:00 pm, and most of the guests had arrived. All the guests were informed previously to be at the hall no later than 7:30 pm, to avoid any stragglers that might spoil the surprise.

Joey stopped by the hall about 7:15 pm to make sure everything was going smoothly. It was planned that Joey would pick up Yvette and take her to the hall.

After he picked her up, he told her that they were going to Jonathan's Hall, and that he rented the hall for the two of them to have dinner there; someone special would have dinner prepared for them exclusively. All the while she was thinking, what the surprise could be and who would be cooking for them. Little did she know the surprise was on a much grander scale.

She asked him, "Why are we having dinner at Jonathan's Hall?"

He replied, "I don't want to do the traditional dinner like everyone else at a restaurant full of people. I want us to be alone."

From the look on his face, she was convinced that Joey was sincere in what he was saying. So she left well enough alone.

He told her how beautiful she looked, and that it didn't take much effort because she was already attractive.

Yvette smiled with shyness, and with a soft voice, she said, "Thank you, baby. I can tell that this is going to be an adventurous evening, happy birthday to me!"

Joey reached out to take her hand and told her how lucky a man he is as he makes this statement, "If you don't be careful, I might ask your hand in marriage as we move forward."

At this time, she turned a couple of shades darker, blushing, as they head to their destination. Once they were there, Joey got out of the car and opened the door for her and she politely said thank you. He proceeded to take her hand again, closing the car door, and escorting her down the sidewalk. Joey parked in front of the hall because the remainder of the cars were parked at the back and out of sight from them.

Once at the door, he opened it and let her go in first. Once inside, the crowd came out of nowhere and shouted, "Surprise!"

Yvette was startled by the loud voices that rang out simultaneously. She then hit Joey in the chest and said, "I should have known you were up to something!"

She pulled him toward her and kissed him on the lips and said, "You, devil." Then, she grabbed her mouth in excitement when she saw how lovely the place was decorated.

Yvette proceeded in the direction of the crowd, still holding her mouth with one hand and the other reaching out to greet her unexpected guests, as tears rolled down her face.

CHAPTER 6

Feliz Navidad

It was the night before Christmas, and all through the house, not a creature was stirring, not even Tony, Bobby, or Joey. They were all sleeping. The three of them hung out last night with some of the other guys from school. Brian hosted a poker party for whoever wanted to attend. He set it up where all who wanted to participate would have to buy in at twenty dollars and receive that amount of poker chips. They could purchase more if they chose.

Brian provided the food and the drinks. It was a pretty good turnout; about twelve guys showed up. He had the party in his basement while his parents visited his dad's brother in Texas for the Christmas holidays. Brian had the house to himself for an entire week. The party went on until the next morning, and this explained why the trio was still sleeping.

Tony got a call from Cheryl about 3:00 pm that same day to remind him to get ready for the drive they were going to make. They made plans to meet the others at the cabin which was three hours away. Tony did not answer his phone right away because he was sleeping, so Cheryl left him a message to call her back when he received the message. Well, about an hour later, he called her back.

"Did you enjoy yourself with the fellas last night?" Cheryl asked him.

He replied, "You mean this morning?"

She said, "Tell me that you all didn't stay up all night?"

"Yes, we did," he replied.

"Well, I answered my own question. Yeah, y'all had fun for sure!!"

She went on to say that she was calling him to remind him about the trip that they were going to take, and both of them had to be there the following day. Tony reassured her that he had already packed and had not forgotten about the trip.

About 9:00 am the next day, they both headed out to the cabin. Joey and Yvette as well as Bobby and Jackie met them there. They all planned to be together for the Christmas holidays. It was very fortunate that the cabin was acquired by Bobby's grandparents who had time-shares in the property. His grandparents were there also, they arrived a couple of hours later. They stopped to pick up the Christmas tree.

Bobby was given a key the night before so that he and the others didn't have to wait for his grandparents to get there. The trio did almost everything together, and celebrating Christmas was nothing short of this. The three of them and their significant others had planned this trip for two months.

Every couple had their own room. The cabin was huge. It had a floor plan that was every bit of 7,000 square feet with a full kitchen, a terrace, two fireplaces, a patio with a full-size grill, and six bedrooms with their own bathrooms, to accommodate the guests. The area was secluded, the nearest cabin was close to four hundred yards away.

The outside of the cabin was built of wood and stone. The architect did a wonderful job on its design and structure. It was unique and beautiful. The landscape with the trees and the snow was breathtaking . . . just imagine! The first night in the cabin, they all pitched in to decorate the Christmas tree. It was all hands on deck.

Christmas carols were sang as well. Afterwards, everyone participated in watching a movie while chowing down on finger foods. This was a quick and easy way to prepare for something to eat. They cuddled up with the one they cared about and watched a good action-packed movie before it was time to turn in for the night. The following morning, the women cooked a big breakfast. This was everyone's chance to experience homemade biscuits prepared by Bobby's grandmother. (Yeah, the ones that he would often talk and brag about.)

The men went outside and collected wood for the fireplace. While collecting wood, they would tell jokes to pass the time. Bobby's grandfather went with them. When the guys got back to the cabin, they got the fire going before they all sat down and had breakfast.

The fire was prepared early so that it would be nice and warm when they all got back inside from the outdoor activities they were planning on doing. Everyone had gone outside to enjoy the wonderful creation that God made. They competed with one another to see who could build the coolest-looking snowman, the men versus the women. This lasted for a little while. The grandparents shouted, "Who wants ice cream?"

In perfect harmony, they all answered, "We do!"

So the grandparents parted ways from the younger ones and collected snow to make homemade ice cream. The youngsters continued having fun by themselves by engaging in a snowball fight.

Later that night, they planned on having a fish fry and play board games. Bobby's grandfather Phil prepared the burner and got the oil hot, while the ladies helped Bobby's grandmother Susan prep and season the fish. There was also tossed salad and fixins' to go along with the meal. The guys helped Phil until he no longer needed their help they then start a poker game while the fish was cooking. They all continued to enjoy the evening.

The next morning, after breakfast was over, they all got ready to pick names for the gift exchange. The women had planned for everyone to purchase a twenty-dollar gift that was coed so that it could be interchanged. It depends if you select a male or female to exchange with. The names would be selected once they got back inside the cabin. Although everyone had purchased gifts for their significant other, they planned this so that everyone could exchange among one another without spending a lot.

It is now Christmas Eve, all the gifts were placed under the tree earlier that day. That afternoon, Susan started to prep the turkey, and the rest of the ladies also helped with slicing, dicing, cutting and rinsing the vegetables. They baked the cakes and pies and prepared other dishes so that when they got up the next morning on Christmas Day; all they had to do was put the ham and turkey in the oven.

Once this was done, the ladies got out the good linen and silverware and set the table. In the meantime, the guys were playing poker again until the ladies were finished setting the table. When the ladies did finish, they joined the men. The men agreed to play a different game of cards so that everyone could play. There were mixed drinks and wine served. Bobby's grandparents knew that they were under age and has taken into consideration how far away the cabin is from civilization. So as long as no one left the cabin driving, they were OK with the teens drinking. Everyone agreed to this, and the fun began.

December 25, Christmas Day! The first ones up were Susan and Yvette. Susan did the last of the prep work and put the ham and turkey in the oven, while Yvette started cooking breakfast. One by one, bodies started slowly showing up in the kitchen when they smelled the aroma. After breakfast was over, while still in their pajamas, they started to exchange gifts. There were a lot of oohs and aahs as they opened them one at a time. Bobby paused and said, "Hang on a minute."

He grabbed his coat and hat and headed for the door. Everybody looked at him surprisingly.

Jackie said, "What are you doing?"

"I'll be back," he said. "I left something in the car."

He reached for the doorknob and went outside. A couple of minutes later, he came back in and had two gifts in his hand. Jackie did not know that the gifts were in the car because Bobby hid them in the trunk. He handed one of the gifts to his grand-mother and the other one to his grandfather.

Bobby said, "I understand why you all are looking so puz-zled. I am giving you both these gifts because I love you both dearly. I have not been the most sensible grandson, and you both stepped up when I lost my mom and dad." Bobby was overwhelmed with emotion. Tears rolled down his face! He continued, "You keep me honest, gave me hope and disciplined me when I needed it. Especially you, Grandpa. You all taught me morals, sheltered me, prayed for me, taught me to respect others, taught me how to reason, taught me responsibility and taught me how to love. I deeply appreciate you both for not giving up on me. You both have made me the man that I am today."

He grabbed them both and hugged them with a strong grip.

By this time, everyone was in tears including Tony and Joey. Yvette joined in causing a domino effect. They all came together hugging each other. Bobby said, "Now open your gifts," and they did. He bought them fourteen-carat gold his-and-her watch sets with his mother and father's names engraved on the backs.

CHAPTER 7

Graduation

Finally here, the seniors can let down their hair and give a big sigh of relief. Yes! No more essays to write, no more study hall, no more exams. No more anything associated with high school! Bobby and Tony wanted to get a clean haircut at Cliff's barbershop, so that they could be presentable when walking the stage to receive their diplomas. Joey got a cut as well, although he would be graduating the following year. He had to groom himself as well. He was going to support his brothers by attending the graduation.

Everyone in town knows that when you go to Cliff's barbershop, it's first come, first serve. The only time that the shop was not crowded and you did not have to wait long was in the mornings. Everyone knew this as well, but the advantage goes to the one who gets up early enough to claim his spot. There were four chairs to choose from, and with those chairs, there were four barbers who had their own unique way of cutting. So customers could select them according to the particular style of cut they wanted. At Cliff's, the variety didn't stop there. Some barbers were young, and some were seasoned. This barbershop was clean, the barbers were courteous, and they had vending machines there in case you wanted a snack while you waited. They also had a variety of books and magazines to read. Wi-Fi was available too. Cliff made sure that his customers were comfortable by all means.

Joey showed up before Tony and Bobby. There was a customer that got there before him, so Joey had to wait until he was finished. He would then be next to sit in Jeff's chair. The person that was ahead of Joey was none other than Robert. He was known as one of the troubled ones from the neighborhood. Although he went to a different high school than Joey, he was still known. Robert was sitting close to Jeff's chair with his earplugs in, pre-occupied with whatever he was listening to.

So when Jeff yelled, "Next," Joey looked around to see if anyone was heading to Jeff's chair. No one did, so he got up, went to his chair and sat down. Joey proceeded to tell Jeff how he would like his style of cut. Ten minutes had passed and that's when Robert noticed that Joey was in the chair. Robert then took off his earplugs and made a couple of rude remarks. Jeff intervened and told Robert that he completely forgot that he was next up, and that he would cut him after he was finished with Joey. He had already started and he would not charge Robert for the mistake he made.

Unfortunately, that was not good enough for Robert. He grabbed his book bag, and full of rage, he headed for the front door, deliberately hitting Joey's leg as he was sitting in the chair. Bobby and Tony arrived and witnessed everything that happened, by this time. Twenty-five minutes later, Joey was done with his haircut and stayed in the shop until Bobby and Tony were done. He had intentionally did this in case Robert was waiting outside for him. It was an intuition thing; he was basing this on the way Robert left the shop in an unpleasant way. Both Tony and Bobby were obviously still in their barber's chair.

Robert did not know that Joey was not alone. Remember, Robert went to a different high school and did not know of the trio and their relationship. So after they all paid their respective barbers and gave them a tip, they headed out the front door. The three of them were not surprised to see Robert waiting outside. This confirmed what Joey had initially thought. Joey drew this conclusion based on Robert's reaction in the shop and the reputation that he had.

Robert was not alone. He had a couple of his goons with him also. Their names were Felix and Ricky. He must have called them on his cell when he went outside. Robert's friends were not with him thirty minutes prior. Robert called Joey out, "Hey, I didn't appreciate you taking my spot in the barber's chair, and that's a problem for me and my buddies."

Joey replied, "You might have heard if you were paying attention. Jeff clearly stated that it was him that made the mistake, and he tried to make it right with you, so there is nothing further that I can do."

Robert said, "I don't care, but there is something we can do."

Robert still didn't know the three were together because Bobby and Tony deliberately stayed back about twenty feet behind Joey, which no one would have expected. People were coming and going, and this could easily be assumed. Once

Bobby and Tony caught up with Joey, Bobby made a statement, "Pardon me while I intervene. He is not alone. As you probably suspected, yes he is my brother, and he tried to reason with you. So here is your instruction! Be wise and let this thing go before it escalates into something you and your buddies might regret. Furthermore, if you're talking to him, then you are talking to us. We are one in the same. Understand that?"

Then, Tony responded, "Yeah, that was good advice, and I think you should take it!"

Robert replied, "Who the hell are you! Instruction? What the hell do you mean instruction! I don't take instructions."

One of Robert's buddies, Felix, said, "We sure don't."

Robert's other buddy, Ricky, stepped in and said his part, and it went back and forth. Although Tony was the last to speak, Robert was still holding a grudge on Joey and mean mugging him most of the time. At the same time that Robert was expressing himself, he took his index finger and poked Joey in his chest.

He got exactly what he was looking for . . . a reaction. Joey hit Robert directly in the jaw with the momentum constant with that of a baseball bat. You could hear something snap like a twig. The other two started to approach Joey at the same time. The fight was on. Everyone had picked a partner at this point. By this time, there were a couple of customers who were headed inside, and they saw this fight unfold. So one of them quickly went into the barbershop and announced, "There are some guys fighting outside!"

All the barbers and customers ran outside to see what was going on. When they went outside, it was total chaos. Jeff, seeing everything as it was unfolding, pulled out his cell phone and called 911. Once the 911 operator answered the call, Jeff told them that a terrible fight was taking place, and that they needed to send the police and the ambulance.

There were signs of bloodstains on the sides of the building and the sidewalks. From the looks of it, it appeared that Joey and his bunch were winning by a lot, if you were keeping score. People were attempting to pull the others apart, but were not successful. It didn't matter though. The police had arrived about three minutes after the call. They arrived first, and four minutes later, the EMTs pulled up. About four cop cars showed up, and there were spectators all around. The cops proceeded to pull them off each other. Bobby and Felix did not submit to the demands that the officer had given. So the officer had no choice but to pull out his Taser and use it. The other officer used his taser as well.

When things finally calmed down, the officer recognized Robert and his goons. The rest of the officers placed the handcuffs on all the parties involved. This was the procedure until the police sorted everything out. Once separated, they took confessions from the guys who were fighting as well as customers and the barbers. When questioned, Jeff told the police what had happened inside which led to the altercation. The police had no doubt that Robert had initiated the fight somehow. This was not the first time he had been in handcuffs and probably not the last. Once the police got all the statements, they concluded that Robert was given a chance to walk away and was offered a free cut, and the fact that he put his hands on Joey first sealed his fate. His buddies were also arrested because they were guilty by association. The police rounded up the three and took them to jail. Tony told the police that the only reason that he and Bobby were involved was because Robert and his friends were planning on teaming up on Joey and were concerned about his safety.

The lead officer told Bobby, Joey, and Tony that they were free to go. He asked the three if they wanted the report sent to them in case anyone asked them about this day. They agreed, one by one, they gave the officers their full names and addresses. He then advised them to have EMS examine them. The three combined had a couple of loose teeth, cuts, and scrapes on their arms, legs, and face. The others did not look so good, they were going to be examined at the jail.

The trio was examined by the EMS, and two of them needed stitches, so they all rode to the hospital together in the ambulance. When they got to the hospital, Joey and Tony received stitches and were released an hour later. They all called their parents and significant others and told them what had happened.

Two weeks later, Robert and his goons had to go to court and face the judge. In the hearing, the judge mentioned to them all, "Every one of you have been in some sort of trouble for quite some time especially you," he called Robert by his last name. "I'm not a counsellor, but I would advise you to get help or change your ways, or you won't live very long at this pace."

He further stated that Robert would be sentenced to five years for this incident and for his prior offences. The other two received three years for their involvement.

After all this excitement, Tony suggested that they go to one of their favorite hangout places and kick back for a while. The place that they were referring to was the old, abandoned railroad tracks close to the old Tinker Cottage building. The trio walked the tracks for about a total of three miles, talking about their version of the fight in detail. This is the place they commonly visited to reflect, laugh, tell jokes, watch the sun set, or just reminisce on the past.

While heading back toward Tinker Cottage, Tony made a suggestion to stop at a small three-acre lake that they would sometimes visit and continue with their conversation. Bobby and Joey were game. While they were walking, they collected various-sized rocks to throw in the lake. When they reached the lake, they sat down on an abandoned bridge that was over the lake. They are now talking about how they met on the playground in elementary school.

Joey took a shot at Tony. "I remember when you walked up for the first time with your blue silk shirt with four-inch collars and a five-inch Afro to match." They all start laughing.

Tony responded, "Yeah, I remember when you had on a muscle shirt, with no muscles in it."

They continue laughing… this went on for a few minutes. The trio also talked about the love of their lives, this went on for a few minutes as well. Bobby looked over at Tony and then Joey and said, "I want to thank you both for being there for me when I lost my parents. I don't even remember making that official to you guys, so if I haven't, then this is the time."

He then balled up his fist and gave each one of them a fist bump and said, "Thanks, bro," to each one of them as his arm was in motion. Tony turned around and said, "You're welcome, bro!"

Tony went on to say, "Do you both realize that we have done a lot of things together, if you think about it, we would always support each other and never had to find companionship in all the wrong places. I have to say, that was quite an accomplishment, wouldn't cha say?"

Joey replied, "You are absolutely correct. We are all that we got."

Tony went further to say, "For us, to be different in culture and color, it's a wonderful thing for us to remain trustworthy and loyal to one another. It's extremely rare. We only judge each other by what we do, not because of the color of our skin."

Joey responded, "You're right. It must be what God intended. I can't think of anything else!"

Bobby then said his piece, "If it wasn't for our brotherhood and closeness, where would we be or how would we have turned out? I want to say one more thing. There is nothing I wouldn't do for either one of you. If you call, I will come running no matter what, and I am confident that you would be there for me. Can we all agree to this?"

Joey and Tony looked at him as though he was going to jump in the lake and commit suicide.

Tony responded, "Really? That goes without saying."

And Joey quickly said, "You didn't know?"

Bobby stated, "Well, I guess that makes this official, I endorse it because I'm the oldest!"

Tony smiled and gave Bobby a fist bump and hugged him. He then turned around and grabbed Joey and hugged him as well; they all were a little teary-eyed.

It was time to start heading home. The hospital instructed them to clean their bandages every few hours. With the hugging and fist bumping, the wounds started to bleed, and it was time to head in, not to mention the sun was going down. The guys knew where they stood among one another with no guessing involved. Now, that's brotherhood at its best.

Four days had passed since the fight broke out, and the three of them were still healing both mentally and physically. It was time to prepare and focus on graduation. Tony called Cheryl and asked her what she thought about going shopping for something nice to wear for graduation. He further mentioned that it would be nice to invite Bobby and Jackie along.

Cheryl replied, "That would be a lot of fun. Better yet, let's make it a full day and include some fun activities to go along with the shopping."

Tony agreed that this was a wonderful idea. Cheryl told Tony that she would call Jackie and make the suggestion and Tony was to call Bobby and see if he would like to participate. Although this was a short notice, they all agreed to meet up the following day at the mall. They met at the front entrance of the JCPenney store around 10:00 AM.

Everyone showed up on time. Once there, they decided to separate in twos and meet in the same spot at JCPenney three hours later. Bobby and Jackie went to a variety of stores and picked out several outfits and tried them on asking the other which outfit looked the best. Jackie did ask Bobby for his opinion, but told him that she wanted to finalize this with Cheryl, being a woman and all. Bobby was OK with this. He went on to say, "It doesn't matter, whatever you choose will look good on you anyway!"

He told Jackie that he was speaking the truth, and he was also trying to build some points.

Jackie laughed at him and said, "I need you to calm down because your day will come soon enough. We will be together after the graduation."

Bobby smiled with excitement. Cheryl and Tony were going from store to store as well, having their own little fun. Three hours had passed, and they all met up together as planned. Jackie showed her outfit to Cheryl and told her that she needed her approval and that Bobby's opinion was OK but not great. She needed a woman's opinion. Cheryl laughed and then looked at Bobby noticing his reaction.

It was lunchtime and they were trying to decide where they were going to eat. Jackie had come up with several choices: seafood, soul food, Italian, burgers, pizza, Mexican, or Chinese. The four of them decided on Mexican food so that they could take advantage of the unlimited virgin margarita specials that they were serving until 3:30 pm.

When they arrived at the restaurant, the conversation was about graduation and how exciting it would be to walk the stage to receive their diplomas. The conversation was also about high school itself, how much fun they had throughout the years and how much they were going to miss being with one another. They all held their glasses up and made a toast to the senior class.

Tony led them, "I want to thank all of you for your encouragement and support, the teachers and staff for their involvement and guidance, my football coaches and fellow teammates. Here's to the senior class of 1996!"

It's May, and graduation day has finally arrived. All the seniors scrambled around... getting themselves ready, prepping and preparing. The graduation was to take place at 2:30 pm on Saturday, May 23. Although Joey would not graduate with his buddies, he and Yvette still attended the event. Yvette would graduate from her high school that following Saturday, the 30th of May. All her friends from various schools would support her on her special day as well.

Here we go! The ceremony was set up with the school mascot on display and the school colors covered the entire auditorium. After all acknowledgments of the principal, superintendent, and under classmen, the valedictorian and salutatorian, they then announced the graduation class.

Tony, Jackie, Bobby, and Cheryl were called to receive their diplomas, with anticipation. The ceremony lasted for three hours.

After the graduation was over, they all met at the same place where they would normally meet to boost morale after the loss of a game. This was where the seniors reminisced and said their goodbyes. This time all the seniors were present. However, some of the seniors would still see one another because of their relationships, whether it be a companion or a friend or relative. There were a lot of tears and hugs that followed. They did have a senior party that Brian would play host to but not all would attend because some of their families had other plans for them. The trio and their mates continued to hang out until it was time for the party. Most of the class showed up and had a wonderful time. It was close to 10:00 pm. The party was over and the last of the seniors parted ways. Again, hugs and tears were prevalent.

CHAPTER 8

After High School

Young adults, in their late teens… this is where life begins. The trio had gone on and pursued careers of their own. Here are the specifics. Joey didn't know what he wanted to do. His life had turned for the worse after high school. He ventured off and made some bad choices at this point in his life, despite his positive upbringing. He was raised right, but got himself in some bad situations. Yvette did not give up on him, she could not understand what happened to him and why. She tried talking to him, gave him money as he needed it and encouraged him. It eventually got the best of her, so she didn't come around much anymore. She told him that she would be praying for him and would wait for him until he got his life back in order.

Joey got an apartment with a guy he knew from school named Anthony; they fell on hard times. One day Anthony asked Joey, "Wanna make some extra money?"

Joey responded, "Sure!"

So it was set. Anthony told Joey that he was planning on burglarizing people who left their garage doors open. He stated that this was an innocent way of hustling with no one getting hurt. The two of them would steal items like weed eaters, lawn

mowers, compressors, battery chargers, bikes, tools, just whatever they got their hands on. The apartment complex that they
lived in was a bit run-down. The area was not good at all. As a
matter of fact, one day, when Joey went to his small SUV that
he purchased last year (which was beat up because of the activ-
ity that took place while it transported the goods to be pawned)
to get something out of it, there were bullet holes in the front
windshield. This showed the type of area they lived in.

To add insult to injury, they eventually lost their apartment and became homeless. Tony and Bobby gave him money
from time to time. This was the only way they could help him.
Bobby was with his grandparents, and space was limited. Tony
was still living with his parents along with his two siblings. This
was out of the question. This is the reason Joey moved in with
Anthony, his options were limited. Bobby and Tony were not
aware of his extracurricular activities. This is the reason Joey
moved in with Anthony, his options were limited. The stealing
escalated one day, they got pulled over by the police. Lucky for
them, there was not much stolen merchandise in the vehicle
"this time."

They both did some jail time. Now, Bobby, Tony, Yvette,
and his parents knew something was going on. He called his
parents and asked them to post his bail. As a result, everyone
that was close to him was affected. His parents paid the bail,
but now Joey had a felony on his record because of the nature
of the crime. Anthony called his family also and asked them for
bail money. He agreed to pay them back as soon as he could.
Joey and Anthony had no place to stay once they got out of jail.

Joey went to his parents for help. Joey's dad told him that he would never deny him anything to eat or a place to bathe. But the condition was that he and his friend had to sleep in the SUV in the carport. Joey's parents knew Anthony from school and knew he wasn't a bad kid, he just made bad decisions so they both were OK with this. His dad was not a mean person. He just wanted to prove a point and show a little "tough love." His dad called Bobby and Tony and asked them to talk to him, and they did. The talk was firm but also sincere.

Anthony finally got a break, his family helped him by moving him to Atlanta with other family members who could help him better his life. Joey got a wake-up call all his own. He wanted to change his life... or die on the streets. He knew that if he didn't, this would devastate the people closest to him. They dared not to tell his little brothers anything that was going on. Joey had always been a respectful young man. He just made bad decisions all of a sudden.

When Joey watched television, he noticed that the same commercial would come on about the navy and how you could see the world and defend your country all at the same time. Remember, Joey was a person of morals and thought that it would be a good thing to protect his country. Besides, he could see the world for free. That's a win-win. So he thought, *Hell! What do I have to lose?*

He called the number on the screen and made an appointment to meet with a recruiter. A couple of days later, the doorbell rang. It was the recruiter. Joey opened the door and invited him in. Joey introduced himself and his parents. The recruiter sat down on the sofa and pulled out some colorful brochures. Joey's mom asked them if they would like something to eat or drink.

After they responded he turned to Joey and asked him a few questions. One of them was, "Are you afraid of water?"

Joey responded, "No, I know how to swim. I had swimming in PE class for three consecutive years."

"Great," he replied. "We're good there."

He went on to ask him why he chose the navy, and Joey told him the reasons. He also told the recruiter that he had a past, and as a result, he had a record as a felon. He replied, telling him that if he passed the written exam and boot camp, stayed out of trouble and paid his court fees, then he would be good to go. The recruiter gave Joey a compliment stating that he looked healthy and strong. He further asked Joey about his academics in high school and requested to see his transcripts. Joey's father asked the recruiter what exactly was the navy looking for when it came to fulfillment of positions and duties.

He said that they had a few positions on the aircraft carrier for enlisted men and women. He went on to say that they had to go to boot camp for eight weeks, and if boot camp was successful, then they would receive their duties and responsibilities at that time. Once you become a sailor, then you will be given the name of your assigned ranking officer and report to him or her at that time. The good thing about this was that while you're on the ship, you have the opportunity to move up in rank, depending on what you have learned, how much you retain, and the years of service.

Joey's mother was pleased at what she heard. But like all mothers, she was concerned about his safety. The recruiter assured his mother that safety should be the least of her concerns, unless he jumped off the ship. Then, there would be nothing that they could do. They all laughed, this was reassuring to his mother.

The recruiter gave Joey the brochures and asked them if they had any more questions; they did not. Joey then walked him to the front door. He handed Joey one of his business cards and told him to call when he was ready. The recruiter told him that he was in good hands as he was leaving. Joey was sure that this was what he wanted to do. But he could not keep the ones he loved dearly off his mind. Yvette, his parents, his younger brothers, and his buddies. This was a hard decision he had to make. He also understood that he would be able to see them every six months, unless something severe happens and he had to stay out at sea.

Bobby, Tony, Yvette, and the others knew that this was something he wanted to do, so they were not surprised when he decided to enlist. They just didn't know when.

A few hours passed, Joey had made up his mind. He called the recruiter and left a message on his voice mail about the decision. The recruiter did not answer the phone at this time. It was after 8:00 pm. The next morning, he called Joey back, and they discussed the details of his test and when he was to show up for boot camp. Joey had one week to say his goodbyes. He would be leaving Wednesday the following week. He told his parents and his younger brothers later that day. His mom wanted to cook a big dinner for him and asked him to invite Yvette, Bobby, Cheryl, Tony, and Jackie over.

Yvette was the next person he called, Bobby and Tony followed shortly after. It was Tuesday, and dinner was scheduled for Thursday. Yvette drove over shortly after their phone conversation. She and Joey had gone to the store to get him some personal items to pack. Sometimes, he would look at her. He noticed that her eyes were swollen from crying. She was trying to hold them back at times but it was impossible to do. Joey would occasionally give her a hug and tell her that he wasn't going to be gone forever, wiping her tears away.

She replied, "I know, doesn't mean I have to like it!"

On their way back, they stopped at Tony's house to invite him to dinner on Thursday. After they left there, they went to Bobby's and invited him as well. (Remember, they didn't stay far from one another.) Joey's mother cooked a dinner that would leave a lasting impression on all of them. She cooked a pork roast with fresh carrots and potatoes along with some brown gravy and fresh dinner rolls. She also made two cherry cheesecakes that should have won awards. When you walked in the house, you could smell the garlic and rosemary seasonings.

Bobby and Tony each brought a bottle of red wine. Yvette brought some appetizers for them to indulge in before dinner. Once they got to Joey's, everyone had questions. They wanted details of his assignment. Joey's little brothers struggled the most because they just knew he was leaving and couldn't understand, why in their little minds.

Before dinner, Joey went to their rooms and talked to them thoroughly explaining to them what was about to happen. He also assured them that he would be back every six months and for them to expect him. He also told them that once he was back for good, that he would never leave them again. What he did not tell them was that if there was an emergency and he had to stay at sea, then it would be even longer before they would see him again. The little ones understood by nodding their heads.

Jackie and Yvette set the table, while the trio went outside to chat. Tony and Bobby agreed that the dinner was perfect timing for them to get together because Bobby was also going into the armed service. Bobby was planning on going anyway; he made up his mind to pursue his career after ROTC. He would be leaving for the army three weeks after Joey departed. They all planned on doing something they were good at—partying! They made plans to go to the nearby casino the day after and have some fun playing their favorite game of poker and slot machines.

They made a full day of this. Time was limited, so they all made the best of every day from that point forward. On their way to the casino, they planned the days to come.

Saturday, the following day, they grabbed their fishing poles, went to the bait shop, grabbed some fresh bait and some snacks. They headed to the lake. It was about 8:00 am when they arrived. They stayed on the lake until about 3:00 pm. In that amount of time, the guys managed to catch a lot of fish. They went to Joey's house to clean and prepare the catch.

Tony suggested, "Hey, why don't we have a fish fry on Monday in the evening?"

Joey and Bobby replied with a fist bump in agreement with Tony's idea. Joey made special arrangements to spend time with Yvette later that evening.

He and Yvette went to get some ice cream at the local ice cream parlor, then drove to a secluded area. They let down the windows so that the warm air could blow through their hair as they sat and talked while enjoying their ice cream. She told him how proud she was of him and that she understood that it was just a matter of time, before he would find his way; and that she never doubted him. She went on to say that he had to find himself, and the decisions that he made previously were not consistent with his character.

He was very thankful and said, "I would think of you at times and my conscience told me that you loved and cared for me. I know that I had to get it right if I am to have a future at all, especially with you, and praying never hurt anyone."

She blushed then grabbed his hand and said, "You got it."

The evening continued with total romance.

It's now Sunday, the day of worship. The entire family and friends thought it would be a good idea to go to church. It's been a while since they had all gone together. All parties had on their best suits and dresses and were ready to worship. They sang and shouted, feeling the Spirit as it moved them. Prior to the service, Joey's parents spoke to the pastor, telling him that Joey was leaving to serve his country because he wanted to change his life. The pastor responded to them and said he wanted to announce this publicly in Joey's honor and for the congregation to pray together for his safety. Joey's mom loved the gesture and told the pastor how grateful they were.

The service went on for two and a half hours. It was close to 2:00 pm. After the service was over, they all went to this famous country kitchen buffet to eat. Joey's parents paid for the meal. Everyone had gone up to fill their plates full of the different variety of dishes that the restaurant had to offer. Once they all sat down, Norman asked everyone to join hands so that he could lead the prayer and bless the food. When they all finished eating, they parted ways hugging and thanking his parents.

Later that night, the trio and their significant others went to the movies for the last time before Joey left. The evening ended early around 9:00 pm. Most of them had to be at work the following morning.

It's Monday morning, two days before Joey ships off to boot camp. It's about 9:00 am, and everyone in the house had either gone to work or school. His mom made breakfast while he was still asleep. She left some food on the stove for him. After he ate breakfast, he went to the garage and grabbed the water hose, weed eater, lawn mower, a couple of rakes, and some trash bags. He started the day by mowing the lawn, raking the grass, and watering it for his dad so that this would be one less thing he had to do when he got home from work. Joey could tell that he had done a good job on the yard because he received a couple of honks and thumbs-up from the passing neighbors, as they pointed at the yard. Joey felt like he had just received the Nobel Peace Prize.

He finished the yard and as he was putting everything back into the garage his phone rang. It was Yvette calling him on her lunch break. She called him to say hello and asked him if the fish fry was still on for the night. He answered yes and told her that he couldn't wait to see her.

She responded, "Same here, babe. Listen, I only have a few minutes to eat lunch, and you know I have to take advantage of the time that they give us."

He responded, "I totally understand. Well, sweetheart, have a great day, and try not to think of me that much. They pay you to focus on your work, OK?"

She replied, "You're silly! Gotta go. Luv ya."

Joey went in the house and took a shower. He then went to the freezer and took out the fish so it could thaw. Then, he called Bobby and Tony to remind them about the fish fry. He had some free time on his hands, so he decided to play video games until everyone got home.

It's 4:00 pm, and Norman is the first one home. Once inside the house, he called Joey's name.

Joey responded, "Yes, Dad?"

"Wow", "The yard looks great! Did you have something to do with this?" He asked… knowing that he did.

Joey responded, "Hey, Pop, I did it just for you! You can focus on the important things now!"

"Thanks, son!" Phil said. "I really appreciate it."

Joey told his father, "No, thank you for being there for me and believing in me, Dad. It's the least I can do."

They both embraced each other. By this time, everyone had made it home. His mom also noticed the lawn and how beautiful it looked. This was the first thing she mentioned before putting down her purse. After she kissed her husband and children, she relaxed for a moment. Grabbing the television remote and a bag of chips, she set out to watch one of her favorite game shows while reclining in her favorite chair. All those that were inside knew this was her time and understood this very well. So for the first half hour, there was no sewing, cooking, folding clothes, washing dishes, sweeping, or mopping.

The boys went into their rooms. They had a white board in which they kept tally of how many days were left before their oldest brother would depart away from them. They would erase one line at a time until there were no more. Each day grew harder and harder for them to erase. When this was all over, the boys went to Joey and asked him if he could take them to the park and play catch.

Joey said, "Sure. We can go just as long as we make it back before 6:00 pm so we can help Mom prepare for the fish fry. So meet me in front in about fifteen minutes."

The park was conveniently located four blocks down the street. With excitement, Joey's brothers Jacob, and Michael ran to their rooms and changed clothes. They put on old jeans and T-shirts that their mom would surely approve of. Joey told his mom that he was taking the boys to the park. Then he went to the garage to get the cooler with rollers and loaded it with bottled waters. Michael had gone to get the football while Jacob went to get a few clean sweat rags. They all eventually met in front.

The plan was that the fish fry would start close to 7:30 pm. About 5:40 pm, the three of them head home after spending a good amount of time at the park. While they were walking, Jacob made a comment, "We sure are going to miss you, big brother," and Michael agreed.

It was heartfelt and Joey responded, "Well, we still have two more days to spend together including tonight." They both perked up a bit, as they kept walking. When they got home, their dad was setting up the burner and the propane tank on the patio. Their mom would normally fry the fish on the cooktop in the kitchen. But there was a lot of fish, and they were definitely expecting more guests than usual. Joey's mom was in the kitchen cutting vegetables for the salad, washing the potatoes, and seasoning the fish, as she was watching her small television.

The two boys took showers, then they played video games. Neither one of them had homework. Joey took a shower and helped his mom in the kitchen. About 6:45 pm, Yvette showed up. She hugged everyone, gave Joey a kiss, washed her hands, and helped prepare the food as well. The boys were happy about this particular night because they were allowed to stay up longer than usual, on a school night.

It's about 7:05 pm, and the doorbell rang. It's Tony and Cheryl along with Bobby and Jackie. Tony said as he walked in, "Man, you could smell the aroma all the way to the sidewalk in front of the house!"

Ten minutes later, a couple more of Joey's friends from school showed up. Everyone brought something to drink including cold beer. The evening lasted a little longer than usual. Everyone was having a good time. They held their glasses high in the air and made a toast to Joey before food was served. It got close to 10:30 pm and the guests started to slowly fade away, saying their goodbyes as Joey met them at the door.

The boys had gone to bed, so Joey, Yvette, his mom, and dad cleaned up. Joey told his mom and dad that they could turn in for the evening and that he and Yvette would put up the last of the dishes.

It's now a little after 11:00 pm, he walked her to her car. When they get to the car, he grabbed her and stared into her eyes and said, "I'm a lucky man to have you as mine."

She turned a different shade of violet. Holding him close to her, she said, "I'm a lucky woman to have a man, who has a strong will and loves me the way you do."

They both kissed each other. He helped her into her car and closed the door for her. She looked at him once more and put her hand over her mouth, she blew him a kiss, and then drove off. It was only a matter of hours before they would see each other again. She took off work for the next couple of days to be with him.

It's now Tuesday. Joey is the only one home at this time, 9:00 am. Everyone else had gone to work or school. He and Yvette made plans to go shopping for a few items that he needed to pack for his long journey. He took a shower, put on his favorite cologne, a nice pair of jeans and a shirt that revealed his chest and shoulders. This was a deliberate attempt to keep her intrigued the whole time they were together, and it worked.

Yvette picked him up around 10:30 am. When she saw him for the first time that day, she became motionless.

"Well, I'm glad you can't wear that in the service. I would have a problem with any female that came in contact with you."

"Really!" He started blushing and replied, "Don't worry, dear. I'm only wearing this for you."

She sighed, "Thank God!"

They then head out. Joey had most of his things packed, so they had time to catch a movie after all the shopping was over. It was now 4:00 pm when they both arrived back at Joey's. Everyone was home when they arrived. Joey's mom made a suggestion, "Let's order pizza and look at some family photos. How does that sound?"

All were in agreement. Joey told his mom that he and Yvette were going to meet with the others later on that night to shoot some pool and he might not be home until the morning. He and Yvette made plans to spend their last night together after they left the pool hall. Joey was not leaving for boot camp until 2:00 pm the following day, so he was able to do an all-nighter. Bobby and his girl were there, so was Tony and his. They all shot pool, played arcade games, threw darts, drank some cold beer and laughed the entire evening. Remember, they were not going to see Joey in a while, so they enjoyed every minute.

The day arrived. Early that morning, he and Yvette arrived back at Joey's house. No one had gone to work or school, without saying goodbye to him. They just happened to arrive early enough for this to happen. Norman had his video recorder ready on a tripod. It captured all the bitter and sweet moments as there was a lot of hugging and kissing and crying as the family was reluctant to leave for work or school.

"We love you!" they all shouted, and he responded, "I love you all. Mom and Dad, I will make sure I lock up the house and I will call you when I touch down."

Joey had to be at the airport by 2:00 pm, his plane would take off at 3:30 pm. It was a thirty-five-minute drive, so he had plenty of time; Yvette was going to take him. Tony dropped by before he went to work and Bobby showed up as well, to say their farewells. The hugs started all over again.

"Goin' to miss you, bro!" Tony stated.

"Yeah, you better believe it!" said Bobby.

"The feeling is mutual!" said Joey as they all embraced for the last time.

Bobby and Tony embraced Yvette.

"This is the last time I will see you before I leave for the army not long from now," Bobby said.

"You're right. I forgot! You take care of yourself!" she said as she hugged him tighter.

"I'll still be here," Tony said. "And if you need anything, let me know."

With eyes filled with tears, she replied, "Thanks, Tony. I know I can count on you if need be," she hugged him even tighter.

"This is it, fellas. Take care of yourselves. I will keep in touch," Joey said as they all gave a fist bump. Joey went into the house to grab his bags. He loaded them up in the car. He and Yvette went to a famous barbeque joint and had lunch before heading to the airport. Although he had to leave and arrive on base before the day ended to be counted as present, he wouldn't actually start boot camp for another couple of days. He wanted to allow time to get familiar with the base. This was going to be the last hug and kiss of the day as Yvette dropped Joey off at the airport.

"I love you and I'm going to miss you. You better keep in touch!" she said.

"Don't sound as though I have a choice!" he said as he pinched her on the butt. "I love you to, sweetheart and I promise I will keep in touch when I am able to."

He grabbed his bags out of the car as they parted ways. He constantly looks back at her. She stayed there until he disappeared into the terminal.

When Bobby left for the army, he felt that the activities that were held for Joey upon his departure to the navy was honoring him as well. They didn't have to plan anything in addition. He felt that being with the ones he loved was sufficient enough. He was OK with not having his own going-away party. The day before he left, Bobby's grandfather asked him to help him in the garage move some items, so that he could have more room inside. So Bobby said, "Give me a few minutes, and I'll be there."

A few minutes passed, and he went to the garage. This was odd because his grandmother was also there, and he had just seen her in the kitchen.

Phil said, "Well, son, I didn't need help after all. Me and your grandmother have something to give you before you leave for the army and show you how proud we are of you."

Susan had a camera hidden behind her back.

"What cha got, Pop?" Bobby said as he would sometimes call his grandfather.

"Look over in that corner and see."

Bobby could not see what it was right away because whatever it was, it was covered with blankets. So he walked over and uncovered it, "and surprise", they had bought him $400 of some of the best fishing equipment that money could buy; to use when he got back home. The look on his face was indescribable.

"Thanks, Pop and Grandma! Wow!" he said, doing an Indian dance. He reached out to them and hugged them both.

"This just made my day. Wow!" he said. Then, he thought… this is not good. "Hey, I have to wait until I get back to enjoy my new fishing gear or die from anticipation. Thanks, guys, and I mean this. Love you both!"

Bobby spent a lot of time with Jackie in the evenings when she got off from work.

Jackie said to him, "First, Joey, and now you. It's a big pill to swallow; you going to the army and him to the navy only weeks apart."

Jackie loved him dearly but was already feeling the strain of him not being there. He encouraged her to hang in there and that he was planning on them, having a future together. This comforted her for the moment.

"OK," she said. "I do love you with all my heart, and I am looking forward to having a future with you, babe!"

He replied, "Well, it's settled. This is what we are going to do then!"

They hugged and kissed each other for the last time before he headed out.

Unlike Joey, Bobby had to leave very early the next day. He and Tony hung out for the last time.

Tony said, "Damn! I'm losing both of my brothers at the same time!"

Bobby responded, "Bro, first of all, you are not losing neither one of us. It's temporary, bro. Hang in there for now. It's gonna be all right. Just let us do our due diligence to serve our country, and we'll be right back in the groove of things. Just wish us well, bro. Luv ya, man!"

Tony said, soaking it all in, "OK, bro, I love you more! Keep in touch!"

They grabbed each other and held on tight for about forty seconds. This all happened right after he and Jackie parted ways. Bobby's grandmother and grandfather took him to the airport. Once at the airport, Bobby and Phil unloaded his bags while Susan was exiting the car. At this point, they were all standing on the curb.

"Well, bye for now, my wonderful grandparents who I love dearly!" said Bobby.

"We love you, sweetheart. Take care of yourself," his grandmother said while shedding a tear.

"Hey, son," said Phil, "I'm going to miss you, and that's for sure!"

"Me too, Pop," and they all grabbed each other at the same time, similar to a huddle; the tears started to stream down their faces. Bobby broke loose from them and headed for the terminal, waving the entire time, he disappeared into the crowd wiping his face. Ironically, he was stationed in California, at a well-known army base. This was a major life changer for him, not only because of the environment, but the climate as well.

While in the army, there were challenges that he had to face. His superiors experienced his rebellious demeanor. The sergeant would give him commands, and Bobby would feel challenged by them. Eventually, he realized that he had to deal with his superiors, just like his experience with his grandparents when he was younger. Being in the army was one of the best things that happened to him. It taught him discipline and how to deal with authority. With the challenges he has ahead of him, he will be thankful for this. He was glad that he endured rather than quit, for he realized that it would do him some good moving forward. Bobby was in ROTC while in high school so he had the experience as to how the army would be and what to expect. So when he joined, he already went in having established a rank. As time passed, he continued to write home, keeping in touch with his grandparents, Joey, Tony, and Jackie as often as he could.

Months passed, and he started noticing that the responses from Jackie were far in between. This was a bit odd to him. Thinking back to the day when he actually left, was when he noticed that Jackie was doubtful and unsure of something. This was consistent to what he believed. He knew that she would miss him and he would miss her. This was expected though. This was why he comforted her the last time he saw her. It had been eight months since he'd been gone. He never stopped writing her. He even tried to call her the very few times he was able to use the phone. One day, he was successful. He actually spoke to her. They both conversed for about twenty minutes. He noticed some cracking in her voice as she was talking.

"What's wrong?" he asked.

"I miss you dearly and I don't exactly know of my insecurities and have not found an answer. I decided to move on," she said.

He just stood there with phone in his hand; as though he was shot in the chest or someone had just tore out his spine.

"Jackie, what happened, sweetheart? I . . . I . . . I don't understand! I . . . What have I done or not have done? Am I to blame?"

"No! You are a good man, it's me not you."

He just stood there. The conversation had gone on for a couple more minutes and they both said their goodbyes. Puzzled and heartbroken with his eyes puffy, he slowly walked back to his barracks. Well, the correspondence eventually came to an end. She did not respond at all at this point. Jackie was seeing someone else, but didn't know how to tell him. For a couple of months, he was to himself for the most part. He did have a confidant that he bunked with to whom he would open up to every now and then. This person kept him hopeful. Praying also helped him to keep his sanity.

He reached out to Joey and Tony. The news struck them as though an 8.5-magnitude earthquake had just happened. They both informed him that they were there for him at any cost. They encouraged him to stay in the army and finish his career because this was just a chapter in his life that he had to file away and not to let this matter go from bad to worse. He had his whole life ahead of him once he finished his duties to serve. Bobby let the advice that he was given by two of the most influential people in his life saturate in his mind. They were right, he thought.

A couple of days passed and he was feeling much better, although she was constantly on his mind. He convinced himself to keep moving forward despite his breakup or breakdown, depending on how you look at it. To add insult to injury, he recently got his orders to go to the Middle East.

Bobby was in the infantry. He spent two years there. He and his fellow soldiers did not get much sleep. They would sleep, taking turns while the others were on lookout, rotating five hours at a time. They were obviously in hostile territory. The team that he was a part of was selected by their major, which means something in the army. Bobby and the team did not trust many people. They endured some of the worst conditions any human would consider inhumane. They had a few challenges: how they relieved themselves the food that they ate, the weather, hygiene, their mental state, being away from home, missing their loved ones, being in a foreign land miles away and who was friend or foe.

Sometimes there would be altercations with the enemy to the point where some on both sides were shot, stabbed or even killed to preserve the way of life; Bobby had his share. The team would be on foot patrol for several days and would get relief from other teams that fit the criteria of being the best; while the previous team would go to the main camp for several days and so on.

At camp, the soldiers had what they called R & R (rest and relaxation). This is where they would shower and shave, eat a decent meal, play games to keep them occupied, read books and magazines, or write letters to loved ones.

All troops that were at the camp were secure 100 percent. It was secured with land mines surrounding them, tanks on the perimeter, thirty-foot manned towers with .50-caliber machine guns, fighter jets patrolling the skies, enough lighting to light up a soccer field, barbed-wire electric fences, and radar. They had peace of mind while relaxing. The soldiers had the responsibility of breaking down their weapons, cleaning them, and reassembling them. This was mandatory of them all, and if someone struggled with this, the others would show them the proper way.

After the fighting died down, Bobby's team had orders to return to the States. It was a long thirteen-hour flight; you could imagine what the troops were anticipating when they got home. I'm sure this was one of many things that crossed they're minds. Watching their favorite team play a competitive game while having cold beer in a mug; so cold that you couldn't hold it in your hand for long.

Although they returned, their responsibilities had not changed. They still had to get up in the early mornings and do drills and stand by on eight-hour shifts in case they were needed again. The good thing of this is that they would rotate on the weekends for R&R, so that no one was deprived. This time, the amenities were different and they were able to live like civilians on the weekends.

This was Bobby's weekend for some relaxation. He drove to Los Angeles and got lost in the big city, doing things to keep him occupied and keep his mind off his parents. Even though he had lost them at an early age, they would pop up in his mind every now and then. Rightfully so, they were his parents. He had completely gotten over Jackie by this time. He eventually found his way to the pier and had some drinks. He would make small talk with the locals and play pool at the local sports bar on the pier. Again, he wasn't very social. Small talk was all he had grown to know.

One day, this all changed when he noticed a slender girl looking his way, more than once. He hadn't noticed it right away, so he kinda watched from the corner of his eye. He was gauging how often she looked in his direction. Sure enough, it was confirmed. Yeah, she got his full attention. She was not a bad-looking gal. About 5'8" petite, yet she had curves that would attract any man's attention. She caught his attention first. She looked as though she weighed about 140 pounds and had black spiked hair, and wearing a T-shirt with a team logo on it; perhaps her favorite team. With heavy starch in her jeans and low-heeled shoes, a medium tan on her skin, she was quite attractive.

She gestured him to come over to her, and he gladly accepted. Bobby introduced himself and asked her what her name was. At once, she told him. He replied that her name was as beautiful as her appearance. Stacey was her name. She was soft-spoken. As they furthered their conversation, he realized that she had a rational understanding and was levelheaded, which was to him another, turn-on.

He then made a comment to her, "I'm going to assume that you came here alone because you were determined to get my attention. Is it safe to ask if you are seeing anyone at this time?"

"No, I am currently single, so you better move fast!"

She had his full attention at this point. They both talked with each other for a few hours having mixed drinks. It seemed as though this moment might change his life for good, he hoped. He told her that he was in the army and that he was stationed in San Diego and took the drive to Los Angeles to get away for the weekend. Bobby felt comfortable telling her about his parents and some of his life's experiences. He totally opened up to her. This was the right moment and time for him.

Stacey opened up to him also and told her life story. The sun was going down, and Bobby made a suggestion, "Let's go down to the SHACK and listen to some music, unless you have something to do?"

She smiled and said, "If this is an official date, then sure."

His eyes lit up, "Yes! It is."

They both headed a few doors down to club Shack and enjoyed the rest of the evening. After the club closed, they hugged each other. He kissed her on the cheek and exchanged phone numbers. Bobby got a room close to the pier. He did the responsible thing and not drink and drive. Stacey went home. He told her that he had one more day in LA before he had to report back and asked if she had any plans later on that day. It's 2:00 am Saturday morning. He asked if she would like to catch a movie later that evening. She said she had to run a few errands, but she was OK with it.

"It's settled then. Call me when you finish with your errands, and we'll go from there, OK?"

"OK," she replied.

He also asked her to give him a call when she got home no matter the time. He just wanted to know if she made it safely. In her mind, she thought that he was very compassionate and considerate. This was a turn-on for her.

Roughly 7:30 pm was when the two got together. They both were dressed to impress. Bobby got the OK from her to pick her up at her apartment. The movie of choice was a drama, this was decided once they reached the theater. They had their share of popcorn and soda, enjoying the movie and each other. After the movie was over, they headed to a burger joint. The evening was going well; it was about seventy-five degrees with a slight wind blowing.

"This is the perfect evening, wouldn't you agree?" she said.

"Yes! It is, so much so; that I would love to take a drive down the coastline. How 'bout it?"

Stacey agreed once more, "Man, you are full of adventure, and spontaneous. I like that in a man."

They drove down the coastline without a flaw. No one could have asked for a better setting or mood. They pulled over into a safe, secluded area that was facing the ocean with the windows already down, they took in all the fresh air that their lungs would allow them to. Snuggling up against each other, they began to kiss, again and again. Bobby was a respectful man and did not allow it to go any further... not that this would have been a problem. He just did not want to move too fast. He further explained to her that this was not the last time he would see her and that he would keep in touch.

It's close to 11:30 pm and he had to get back to the hotel and get some sleep, so he could head back to the base and get ready for duty call early Monday morning. She understood, so he dropped her back at home, had a few more kisses, and drove back to his hotel. Bobby continued to see Stacey; driving back and forth to Los Angeles when he was granted leave from his commanding officer. Of the many conversations that they had, he did tell her that he lived in Rockford and that he would eventually have to go back.

Bobby stayed in the army for another year. He completed his duties as a soldier. He made one last trip to Los Angeles to spend his last moments with her before he flew back home. Before he left, they both had an extensive conversation about their future together. Stacey was willing to move to Rockford on a transfer from her job, if she could find the same type of work or something similar.

Bobby and Stacey lit up like light bulbs, with the idea that this could possibly happen. They kept in touch the entire time. Both were optimistic somewhat, until a decision was made of the transfer. The plan they talked about eventually did happen. She was granted the transfer and was able to find work in her field, and the rest was history. Bobby was constantly updating his grandparents about his new girl and the circumstances that evolved; the fact that they would get a place of their own, and he would eventually move out. Bobby told them all about Stacey. Don't believe he left anything out. They were eager to meet her. His grandparents expressed to him how happy they were, that he had found someone that he was planning on spending the rest of his life with. They further realized that this would be a smooth and much-needed transition for him. His breakup with Jackie, his going to a foreign land to serve his country, the conditions he faced, and the loss of his parents topped it off.

Tony and Cheryl had a strong, long-lasting relationship throughout the years. She told him that she had applied for school and there might be a possibility that she may be leaving Rockford to attend full time. Also, there was a strong possibility that she would be accepted.

Tony said, "It's going to be a bittersweet moment for the both of us. I have no doubt that you will be accepted."

Cheryl replied, "Sweetheart, I love you with all that I possess, and our relationship doesn't have to end."

He said, "Baby, as much as I would like to believe this, reality tells me that we will eventually part ways... not because I want to, but how often would we see each other? Yeah, something to think about, right?"

She just bawled and said, "You're right, come to think of it." He began to bawl as well.

It was not long after high school that she applied for school at Mississippi State University. She stayed in constant contact with the school and the school with her. The university had academic programs that very few schools offered in this particular field. Mississippi State was one of the best. She forwarded her transcripts to the school a month ago. One day, while her mother was checking the mail, she noticed there was a letter from the university. This was exactly what Cheryl was expecting. Her mom put the letter on the kitchen counter and waited with the rest of the family until Cheryl got home. The family wanted to be there when she revealed the news.

When she finally got home, she realized everyone was in the kitchen. Well, it didn't take long for her to figure this out. Her mother handed her the letter, they both grinned simultaneously. With all watching, she opened it, and the first words of the letter were "After further review, the Board of Mississippi State University has accepted you as a full-time student." The family shouted out loud with excitement. The school was impressed with her GPA and knew she would be a good fit. The process had to go through several channels, she was told. Cheryl would be attending school in the fall. She wanted to leave home a couple of months prior to school starting, so that she could get familiar with the campus and the city she would be living in. In addition, she wanted to have time to find a part-time job to have extra money to support her hobbies and any additional activities that came along. Although her family was well off and paid her tuition, she was responsible.

It is now June and she'll be leaving in three weeks. This was all the time she had to spend with Tony, and they made the best of it. There was no ill will between them. He supported her in her decision. When she moved to Mississippi, she and Tony both kept in touch and remained friends. Both of them struggled in the last few weeks and concluded that life must go on.

While Tony was working at the hardware store, his manager encouraged him to pursue a career in electrical. So he got some information about a well-known apprenticeship school in the area. The cost of the school was reasonable. It's a four-year school, and it was the type of school that would pay part of your tuition if you maintained a good GPA and worked so many hours a week. It was a great program if you were accepted. He thought, *If I go to electrical trade school and apply myself in four years and complete the training, I would be sacrificing a fraction of my life, only to be well off for the rest of my life!*

Tony called the school and asked them what he needed to do to enroll. They told him that he must make an appointment to come down and take the aptitude test, and if he got eighty percent of his questions answered correctly, he would be accepted. He did not hesitate to ask what times were available so he could schedule the appointment. They had an opening at 3:00 pm on the upcoming Thursday, which was three days away.

Unfortunately, Tony didn't get off until 4:00 pm. He made the appointment anyway to secure his spot, and he would talk to his manager to see if he could either come in earlier or work later. Tony spoke to his manager; being supportive of him, he gave Tony the option to work earlier that day so he could make the appointment. He also told Tony how proud of him he was.

Tony arrived at the school fifteen minutes early to mentally prepare himself. His name was called. The instructor gave him instructions about the test, how many questions there were, and handed him a couple of sharp pencils. He had two hours to complete one hundred questions. He had to wait until Monday before he got the results back.

Friday, he worked his normal hours. He was constantly thinking about the results. Staying open-minded and optimistic all through the weekend was nerve-racking so he kept himself occupied the entire weekend.

Monday finally arrived. He was stocking shelves while at work. He received a call around 11:00 am. As expected, it was the school, so he took a moment to accept the call. It was the director. The director told him that he got eighty-seven out of one hundred correct for a total percentage of eighty-three, and he was officially a student. He congratulated him and let him know to expect a beginner's packet in the mail sometime next week.

Tony could not stop thanking the director, smiling the whole time. Once he hung the phone up, he expressed himself with gratitude. "Yes!" he shouted with his fists balled up, swinging them as though he was in a boxing ring.

His manager heard him and went to the back, "You got the results, huh?"

The manager shook his hand and congratulated him. The manager whispered to him, "We have customers." Tony had to contain himself. In his first year, he had an impressive GPA. As time passed, it got more challenging. He's young so he had to learn to prioritize his time by disciplining himself. Staying up late or not doing his homework when he should were some of his challenges. He understood that what he put in was exactly what he gets out, so he was diligent by all means. The balance of hanging out versus studying was extremely hard to choose at times. Once he got into a routine and stayed focused, he would overcome this.

Help arrived while he was in his second year. He met a girl named Vivian who worked at the hospital in the administration's office. He met her at a private party that a mutual friend played host too. She didn't stay long. Tony noticed that she was no longer there, so he asked the friend where she had gone. He had intentions of meeting her, it was unfortunate that the opportunity came and went. The mutual friend called her the next day asking her if she remembered who he was; so that he could let her know that Tony was interested in meeting her, if it were possible. Surprisingly, she did remember seeing him. The friend told her that Tony wanted to give his cell number to her and to give him a call. She did in fact call him.

They talked for a few days and decided to meet in person and make it official. This was considered their first date. Both were sports fans, so they decided to go to a sports bar and have beer and burgers. It went extremely well. They both enjoyed each other's company so well that they planned a second date. This time the idea was to sit down at a nice exclusive restaurant so they could find out more about one another.

As time went by, Vivian grew quite fond of him. She thought that he was: funny, considerate, understanding, mature, clean, unselfish, compassionate, outgoing, ambitious, likeable, respectful, pretty much the qualities a woman expected from a man. She supported and helped encouraged him while in school. As school continued, his grades grew even more impressive as time passed.

Tony was now in his fourth year of school. They have dated for a couple of years and decided to get married. The ceremony was beautiful. It was small but beautiful. The bride was gorgeous in her white custom-made dress, which took five weeks to design and make. It was early in the afternoon when they got married. After the wedding was over, all the guests gathered outside of the convention center, and everyone was given a balloon. Once announced, they all released their balloons in honor of the newlyweds' new beginning. Soon after, the bride and groom got into the limousine, and they drove away.

The following morning, they took a flight to Las Vegas for their honeymoon. They had the privilege of staying at the MGM Hotel and Casino.

The following year, Tony walked the stage at his graduation. All his and her immediate family, Bobby and Stacey, friends and his manager were all in attendance. Joey would miss the graduation prematurely by four weeks; he would not have completed his service in the navy until after the graduation was over. Joey did send Tony a nice gift to support him even though he wasn't there.

Wearing his canary-yellow cap and gown and his ten-carat gold class ring on his finger made the whole package complete. While in school, he was supported by several of the staff members who helped him along the way. His first-year instructor, his third-year instructor, the office coordinator, and the director of the school chapter, all played a vital role in his success. Tony and one of his fellow classmates gave them acknowledgments and awards during the graduation ceremonies, showing them appreciation. They both wrote speeches to inspire the students that would graduate in the upcoming years. One of the speeches was about appreciation, and the other was about inspiration.

In addition to receiving his diploma, he also received perfect-attendance awards for three of the four years that he was enrolled.

Tony and Vivian lived together in a three-bedroom apartment in a nice community while their new house was under construction. He now had the means to make this all happen. His position and title had changed to electrical foreman, and obviously, his pay had increased substantially. He is now in the construction business.

According to Tony, this was a perfect start to their future together. The timing could not have been better. They both had three children when it was all said and done.

CHAPTER 9

Life

Joey made it back home. Both Bobby and Tony were living their lives. Joey, like Bobby, had taken time to adjust back to civilian life. Joey's life had made a change for the better at the age of twenty-four. He worked in the hotel industry. He started off cleaning rooms at motels making little money. This was OK with him because he realized the potential for growth. He just wanted to learn the business and eventually make his way up.

It didn't take him long. He asked the manager a lot of questions about how to run and operate the business. He learned that the more he knew, the better off he would be. He would stay long hours with the manager and learn how to work the register and counter; greet people, how to schedule staff members, shift changes, manage and secure the profits, order cleaning supplies, reservations, sanitation, and other things that involved hotel management. He was determined to learn so his manager stayed by his side for months. She mentioned that going to school and getting his certification would "seal the deal, if you will" in order for him to be more marketable in the industry.

Joey went down to the local junior college to see if they offered the course in hotel management. Fortunately, the school did offer the course. It would take him four months to complete the course. Joey eventually became a successful operations manager at a well-known food franchise. He quickly advanced, thanks to the long hours he put in to get the experience and exposure from his manager and school. His skills preceded him because normally a person would have to go to school a lot longer to be awarded this type of position. In his case, he displayed his abilities and determination in a short period. The director of the management team was convinced that this was sufficient to offer him the position. He worked a lot of hours.

When he had time off, he would divide his time between Yvette and his younger brothers who were now teenagers themselves. Joey arranged to have outings with both his brothers and Yvette at the same time. Talk about utilizing good time management, this was brilliant. He would schedule the time they would spend together during the day so that he could do things such as; visit the zoo or go to carnivals, amusement parks, movies, arcades, bowling, and the like. He incorporated this time so that the evenings would be left for him to spend with the one he truly adored.

Joey kept in touch with Bobby and Tony by phone. The fellas had lives of their own. They didn't hang out like they used to. They all were working and had families. Joey thought of owning something, something he could show from the fruits of his labor, something he could leave his children if he had any. He thought that some investment property would be great, but then he thought, why not buy investment property and eventually build. So this was the route he decided to go.

He reached out to Yvette, asking her if she wanted to continue being a part of his life, although he knew the answer, he asked her anyway, just to get a response. After she said yes, this was when he revealed that he was looking for a home for them both. He had a family member who was a realtor. He gave her a call, asked her if they could sit down and talk, asking if he could schedule a time and day that would be good for her. Once Joey got in contact with her, they made an appointment that they both agreed on.

They met at an exclusive place. The realtor asked Joey a few questions, such as; where he wanted to purchase, did he want to build or buy preowned, the location, how much he wanted to spend, how much square footage he was looking for, did he want a swimming pool or not, how many bedrooms he wanted, did he want it furnished, did he want new appliances, big yard, small yard, or no yard, how big of a lot he wanted, did he want a basement, etc. The realtor further explained the process, how they do comparisons with other houses on the market so he could have competitive prices of that particular neighborhood and so on. He told the realtor that it was more to buying a home than he had imagined. She explained that it was more to it than that. His credit had to be good, the closing process, the negotiations, insurance, utilities, inspections, surveys, taxes, crime rates, escrow, down payments and security for the home. These were other things that he would have to consider.

Despite all these things, he was still willing to purchase a house. He shared with the realtor that he was in good hands because she knew the ins and outs of buying a home. This would be an advantage to him if she didn't mind advising him as he went through the process. She had no problem helping him. Besides, he was family. So Joey took a few weeks to decide what type of house he wanted, and Yvette helped with making some of the decisions. As time went on, the realtor provided him with brochures of different homes with all the information. They would then select a few, and view them as their schedules would allow them to. It took them about six months before they purchased their first home.

The neighborhood was diverse and clean with nearby shopping on the east side of town. Once the keys were handed to them their eyes glowed with joy and excitement. Well, it was not long before Yvette had to look for furniture and appliances. There was enough trust among them to reveal their salaries to one another. So they opened up a joint checking account so that they could accomplish this. Joey constantly told her that she was the one he chose to be with for the rest of his life. He also told her that the house was the first step, and it's an honor pursuing this with the one, you care about.

Marriage was in due time. There was no doubt that this would happen, he told Yvette. Some people lead others on, and that was not his intention. He made Yvette understand that it was in this order: (1) house, (2) marriage, (3) children, this is what he wanted because the real estate market was good. He wants to take advantage while he could.

Yvette was very pleased that it was broken down for her this way, and she let him know that. She liked the fact that he had wisdom and thought things through as opposed to just acting on a feeling, which only leads to destruction. He had done his homework, and this further assured her that he was the one. Being considerate and involved in making decisions on what the couple needs, is what Joey found himself doing for the love of his life. Most men would be okay with what a woman chooses. No, he was actually involved in every step of the process because he wanted to do this along with her. Life was good for the both of them.

Bobby had started a new life of his own, which was very similar to Joey's. Fresh out of the army, he found the woman he wanted to spend the rest of his life with as well. He introduced Stacey to his grandparents for the first time, and it went well. They loved her demeanor, compassion, and personality. They knew that Bobby wouldn't just choose anyone, so they expected nothing less when they finally met her. Stacey and Bobby stayed with the grandparents for a while.

Their grandparents had another house that they owned, but it needed some work. It sat up for about six years uninhabitable. Bobby had previously asked Phil in a letter he sent while in the service if he had any intentions to keep the house. His grandfather told him that it was just sitting there, and he was too old to restore it. He then told Bobby that he would sell it to him for a little of nothing, and of course, he gladly accepted. This was why Bobby and Stacey were living with his grandparents. The house was being completely restored, it was going to take some time to get it like they wanted. They had hired a contractor to do most of the construction.

Bobby, with Tony's help tackled some of the minor electrical work for about four hours a week; installing ceiling fans, track lighting, and landscape lighting, finding time among their own busy schedules. They both would do their part and leave. They were lucky if they could be there at the same time, having conflicting schedules.

Tony had a key to the house, so he could come and go as he pleased. They kept their communication open to track progress by e-mail, text, or notes left at the house. Stacey grew very close to Bobby's grandparents, and the feeling was mutual. She thought it would be odd moving in with them when Bobby first told her of his intentions. She helped his grandmother do most anything, and sometimes she didn't even have to ask. She would prepare dinner to give Susan a break or purchase takeout if she herself wasn't in the mood or had a long day. His grandparents knew she was a keeper.

Stacey was enjoying her new job location. It was different than being in sunny southern California. But she was OK with this. Her biggest adjustment would be the winter months, since she had never experienced them. She had no worries though. She had a supporting cast that would teach her everything there was to know about winter and what to expect. As long as she was with Bobby, it really didn't matter.

Stacy held the title of marketing manager over the public relations department, which she was responsible for in the northwest region. It was a lateral move. She was the marketing manager for the southwest region. The work was similar; she had to only make adjustments for the location and the climate.

Her job title and responsibilities were the same. She did have one perk though. The company did pay half of her expenses when she transferred. Stacey had been with the company since she graduated high school as an intern. They hired her on after she graduated. She was responsible for sixty-five people in that region. She had a healthy salary as well.

Stacey graduated from the University of Southern California with a bachelor's degree in business management. She had good posture, was well-spoken, clean, dressed nicely, educated, considerate, fun, spontaneous, just all around good! People loved to work with and for her.

Bobby on the other hand worked long hours at the gun store. He had a fetish with guns and ammunition. When business was slow, he had the privilege of shooting in the range as long as there were no customers, free of charge. He would also reload his ammo if there were no customers as well as break down his weapons and clean them if there were no customers. Just like Stacey, he had a few perks of his own. Not to mention he could work all the hours his body could endure. While working at the gun store, he had encounters with customers from all walks of life. Let's see, anyone from lawyers, construction workers, registered nurses, janitors, managers, police, undercover agents, bail bond agents, store owners, ex-military, husbands, and wives; would all come to the gun range to shoot. He had the privilege of talking to them. Not only to sell them ammunition or accessories, but educate them as well. He talked about how to obtain a concealed license to carry a handgun for protection.

Bobby was also one of the three instructors who conducted the classes. He learned to be a little more outspoken. He had to be, as he was in the business of assisting people. Bobby knew how to make money on the side by training those who wanted to know how to break down their weapons to clean them. The course did not offer this, so he did this on the side. To make people comfortable and trust him, he told them that he had served in the army and gave them some background. This made the customers feel secure and honored at the same time. He came up with the idea himself. The classes were held at his grandparents' house where he lived. Of course, he asked his grandfather if he could conduct the classes in the garage once a week.

Bobby also told him that the customers had to pass a background check in order to attend the classes at the gun range, and it would be the same customers that would come to the house. Phil was OK with this. This was reassuring to him. This was a plus for Phil because his grandson showed him how to clean, preserve, and oil his guns also, free of charge of course. This was also where Bobby did his reloading of ammunition. He had purchased the equipment needed, as well as the gunpowder, the packing material, and boxes. He would purchase additional shell casings if he wasn't able to salvage enough from the range. He was allowed to keep as much of the shell casings as he wanted as he cleaned the lanes at the range. He loved his job almost as much as he loved Stacey.

One day Bobby called his grandmother and told her that he had gone shopping for a special ring and that he was going to propose to Stacey very soon. She reacted as though she was receiving the proposal. She screamed with excitement. Mind you, he never said exactly when this would take place. Occasionally, Stacey would call him and they would make plans to have lunch together. The good thing about this was the fact that they both had flexible schedules.

Bobby anticipated which days would be slow, and Stacey had long lunch periods if she chose to. She had an assistant that was trustworthy, experienced, and knew her way around the office. She could and would relieve Stacey for as long as two hours. Stacey was only a phone call away and made sure her staff had her contact information. They seized the opportunity of the time spent at lunch to talk about their house, the progress, changes and upgrades.

Bobby told her that there had to be a man cave in the plans. She was not at all OK with this. She thought a man cave was a reason for a man to hide something. Bobby had explained to her that that was not every man's intentions. He let her know that he wanted a man cave simply to have his army memorabilia, load ammunition, and watch sporting events without getting in her way.

She completely understood and apologized to him. She said she was a little jealous but now realized there was no reason to be. On one of their lunch outings, he planned for them to go to the park and talk about their future. They met up at the picnic table during a time when the park was not overwhelmed with people. She was looking absolutely stunning, as usual. He brought lunch for the both of them.

Bobby asked her to sit down, and she thought this was odd because he never says "sit down." So she put her purse on the table and complimented how beautiful the day was and thanked him for the food. He asked her if she was done with ranting on about this and that. He reached in his pocket and handed her a small box. Her eyes lit up! She asked him what all this was about, and he told her to open it. Well, she did, and to her surprise, it was a beautiful ring. Waiting for her to get her composure together, he then asked her to marry him. Tears fell down her face in pure joy and excitement. Although she could barely get it out, her response was yes. She could not contain her tears; even after fifteen minutes, the tears would come and go as reality kicked in.

Bobby held her for a period of time and told her how happy he had become. He too shed a few himself as he thought about his parents and wished they were there at this moment and time. She asked him why he was so emotional. He told her how lucky he was to have her by his side and that his parents were in his thoughts. They both comforted each other. She told him that she was extremely happy, but it was unfortunate that when she got back to the office, she'd look a mess... her makeup was ruined.

Bobby let her know that when her staff heard about the proposal, it wouldn't even matter at that point, they will be excited for them; Again, he was right. This had gone on for the majority of the lunch, so they didn't have a lot of time to eat. Thank God Bobby bought sandwiches and chips from the sandwich shop. If he had done anything different, the food would have been cold. Before they both headed back to their respective places of employment, he took the ring and put it on her finger, so she could show off her three-carat pear-shape and platinum diamond ring for all to see. Life was good for both of them. There was no doubt.

Stacey made it home before Bobby, so she was the first to tell her new grandparent-in-laws the good news. She thought about waiting on him, but her emotions told her different. Once she revealed the good news to them, Susan immediately burst into tears. She knew this would happen long before Stacey had known. His grandfather grabbed Stacey and told her that he knew she was the one.

Bobby and Stacey got their start, and neither one of them faltered. It was time to have a future together. The couple stayed with the grandparents for another two months for a total of seven months. The house was ready to move in. There were just a few cosmetic things that had to be addressed, but for the most part, it was ready. They spent their last weekend with the grandparents.

That Friday, the two of them showed their appreciation by taking them to an upscale restaurant, fifty-dollars-a -plate type of restaurant. Having drinks to begin, Phil proposed a toast to his grandson and new granddaughter. Stacey shed more tears when he made the announcement, thinking of the honor that was to come from such beautiful people. They all enjoyed each other as the day turned to night.

What a beautiful day it was to move. They hired a moving company. Most of their friends and extended family had plans that particular weekend. When Bobby and Stacey walked into their newly renovated home, they both sighed with relief. With the fresh smell of paint, it sparked up nostalgia. The house had natural light exploding through its windows. The interior lighting was beautiful. The flooring was just gorgeous. The kitchen and master bedroom and bathroom were breathtaking. The exterior and the landscape were immaculate. The whole house was just simply amazing.

Holding each other, the wonderful gestures they had and thoughts that entered their minds were signs of pure joy and happiness. This was their home. This was a wonderful start for them. God is good!

Bobby called Tony and told him how beautiful the lighting was and how much he appreciated him. Although Tony did not accept any pay from Bobby other than purchasing the fixtures and material, he let Bobby know that it came from the heart. Fact is, he would do the same for him.

Tony had a big responsibility. Being a foreman, he had fifteen other electricians that were on his team. Among the fifteen, they had different levels of experiences. Some were journeyman, and some were apprentices with various years in the trade. He had to assign them to different tasks according to their skill level and capabilities. Talk about busy. He also had to deal with men who had different personalities and age differences. The younger men were sometimes irresponsible. They would sometimes forget their tools or their boots or safety equipment. There were other times when they would be late or be on their cell phones while working. Disciplining them was what he had to do. Remember, they were electricians, and they had to pay attention at all times; there would be times that they may have to help a journeyman with a task and could be exposed to live circuits. Tony would always prepare them mentally to act as though electricity was always present, even when it wasn't. Exercising this would keep them alive.

He motivated them, educated them, and encouraged them. The ones who really wanted to learn or apply themselves, he would encourage them to go to trade school. Those who were very serious, he would give them references to the school that he graduated from. The older electricians pretty much were dead-on. The biggest thing with them is the fact that they had families and would sometimes have to take off work or get emergency calls to tend to their children, this was expected. The down side to this was when there was a construction schedule, he had to postpone; in some cases because his most experienced men were absent for all the right reasons. He understood this firsthand. He too had these things happen to him. All in all, he would make it all come together as a team, and his job became easy because he gained the respect of the men, and he in return had respect for them. But all understood who had the last word. For the most part, they didn't veer out of their lanes. There were a few times when he had to issue verbal warnings, and only two times he had to give written reprimands.

Tony had his work cut out. He wrote his daily reports to the general foreman, about the progress of the job. Working long hours, he and his boss would look at blueprints, order specific materials to complete the task that's scheduled, record time, go over first-aid procedures and emergency drills etc. He attended the meetings that were mandatory once a week. This was company-wide. Occasionally, the estimator would ask Tony to help him bid on potential electrical work for future projects. This was an honor.

He was very busy during the weekdays and would very seldom work on a Saturday unless there was a deadline to meet or a special project that needed to be completed. Other than that, the remainder of his time was spent with Vivian and the children. Vivian worked long hours at the hospital in the admissions department. She also worked Monday through Friday. Both Tony and Vivian spent lots of time with their children. They went to amusement parks, zoos, swimming pools, movies and family reunions. They occasionally traveled out of town during the major holidays as well. During the weekdays, later in the evenings, while the family had dinner or had a little downtime, they sat down and planned the upcoming weekends.

This particular weekend, they made plans to go camping. This was an event that was quite unique because Vivian did not like anything outdoors, let alone camping. The thought of sleeping on the ground with snakes and animals close by was not her idea of having fun. But she made an exception since one of her sons was in the Cub Scouts. Although this did not involve the Cub Scouts directly, he had some outdoor experience that he could share with his mom to ease her mind, assist, and educate her and the rest of the family.

He was knowledgeable about the environment and the animals. Knowing the different animal tracks and how to start a fire with no matches was essential. He also knew what type of plants were poisonous and which ones were not. Tony was responsible for calling the camp grounds and reserving a spot, as well as the camping equipment and rentals. Vivian was responsible for the food, cooking utensils, and personal items. Tony had called a week prior, so there were no issues once they got there. The family packed a variety of things that were needed for camping. Off they went making the four-hour drive to the campgrounds. In the forest was where they'll spend the rest of that weekend. Ooh, what fun they had, with mom screaming and all!

CHAPTER 10

Joey's House

Obviously the trio had lives of their own. What little time they did have, was spent with either their spouses or children. They didn't have time to spend with each other, so life had to go on. Don't get me wrong. They always kept in touch with one another. This would all change though.

Yvette was eligible for two weeks of vacation. She planned on seeing her only sister, whom she hadn't seen in close to three years. She lived in New York. Yvette planned on visiting with her and her family for a week and spend the last week with Joey when she got back in town. She purchased a round-trip plane ticket earlier that month. She was leaving on a Thursday and would not be back until that following Friday morning, which was when Joey would be picking her up from the airport. He had known all along that she had made these plans, but they quickly left his mind.

He was working so many hours that it was hard to keep track of the days. He thought hell, this would be a perfect time for him and the fellas to finally get together. After he got off work, he called Tony first and told him that Yvette was going on vacation and flying to New York. He then called Bobby and told him the same thing. Although the trio had kept in touch, he failed to mention this to them early on. He asked them both to put any current plans aside so that they could hang out together over his house. Mind you, it was just Yvette and Joey who lived together with no children. It was the perfect plan. Bobby told Jackie to make plans of her own for Friday night because he had the opportunity to hang out with the guys.

In the meanwhile, Tony gave Vivian a very similar request. As a matter of fact, Vivian let him know that it was much needed because it has been a while.

The three of them confirmed the plan and put it into action. The plan was to meet at Joey's house Friday night at 7:00 pm. Joey took Yvette to the airport Thursday. He helped her with her bags and set them on the curb while the bellhop checked them in. They both held each other for a good two to three minutes saying their farewells. She told him to have fun, and demanded that he did. He smiled and proceeded to tell her that he loved her and told her to enjoy herself as well, making sure to tell her sister and the family he said hello and that he would see them on the next go-around. He then headed to work. She stood on the curb looking in his direction until she could no longer see him. She continued by making sure that all her bags had claim tags on them. Then, she grabbed her carry-on and headed for the terminal. She sat down at a coffee shop and grabbed an espresso, thinking about Joey and how much she cared for him and how much she would miss him. She was almost in a daze as she was stirring her espresso in a counterclockwise motion.

When Friday came, Joey worked a few hours and clocked out. He called Bobby and asked him if he could leave his job early and meet him at the bar to have a couple of shots before the real party began. Bobby told him that he was all for it, and that he could afford to take off early with no questions asked. Furthermore, one of his coworkers owed him a favor. It was a bad thing that Tony could not have joined them. He did not have flexible time, being in charge of an entire crew, with his responsibility… they didn't even bother.

Bobby and Joey met up at the sports bar around 4:30 pm. Joey got there first and found a couple of seats close to the television. He grabbed a menu, checking to see what he could order to put in his stomach before he did any drinking. The server went over to him and asked him if he needed a minute to look over the menu. He told her to give him a few minutes and that he was expecting one more person.

Bobby arrived ten minutes later. He called Joey to see what part of the sports bar he was sitting in. When he confirmed where he was sitting, Bobby headed over to him, and they greeted each other with the usual fist bump or hug. Joey was concerned that the server took awhile to get back to his table so they could order. So he went to the bar to order a couple of shots for him and Bobby, while Bobby gazed at the menu. Joey purchased the shots and went back to their table. They ordered some cheese sticks and wings to hold them over. They made a toast and turned up their shot glasses. Bobby then went to the bar and ordered two more shots, and they repeated this several times.

They ate and caught up on lost time. It's now close to 6:00 pm, they called Tony to see if he was still at work.. Tony had left the job, but had to go home and take a shower. He told them that he would just meet them at Joey's house at 7:00 pm as planned.

Now everyone was on the same page.

Bobby and Joey leave the sports bar. When they got outside, Joey told Bobby that he was going to stop at the convenience store before heading home. Bobby followed Joey to the convenience store, and they both went in, grabbing a case of beers, some chips and salsa, some peanuts, and a couple of scratch-off lottery tickets. They leave the store and make their way over to Joey's.

They both pulled up in the driveway and went through the back door. Bobby took two beers out of the case and put the rest in the freezer while Joey grabbed two bowls, one for the chips and the other for the peanuts. Tony showed up shortly and rang the doorbell.

Bobby goes to answer it. Once again, they grab each other and give the necessary fist bump. By this time, Joey comes out of the kitchen, and he's yelling, "What's up, bro?" as he reaches for Tony. He then tells them both that they were at home away from home, and it was great that they were all together again. This was the first time that Tony and Bobby had been to the house. Joey tells Tony to grab a beer so he could show them around. Afterward, they all went back into the front room and talked about current events and how life was treating them. Joey then turns on the television to watch a basketball game while they continue to talk more. They all watch the game until halftime starts.

Bobby and Joey are feeling a good buzz by now. Joey looks at Bobby and asks him if he would like to do something daring. Both Joey and Bobby loved to live on the edge. The military was the cause for this behavior. Bobby says sure, and they head for the back room. Tony thinks nothing of this, knowing how radical they both were. There is no telling what they had in mind, so he just stays in the front room and flips through about fifty of about three hundred channels, changing back and forth to see if halftime was over.

When they get to the back room, Joey tells Bobby that he would like to show him something. Joey goes to a dresser that had three drawers on it and pulls out a chrome .357 Magnum with a beautiful wooden handle.

"Damn! That's nice," says Bobby, so he asks to hold it. At the same time, he asks Joey what the dare was. Joey replied asking him if he wanted to play Russian roulette with the gun in a spin the bottle kind of way. Bobby tells him that's his kind of game.

So Joey goes into the garage and gets a couple of foldout chairs and explains the objective to him. He takes all the bullets out of the gun except one and lays the remainder on top of the dresser. He spins the barrel with the one in it, not knowing if it's in the chamber or not. He further explains that who's ever turn it was, he would spin the gun on top of the dresser and wait to see whom it stops on. The person that it stops on has to point it at their head and pull the trigger. They both would have three attempts. So they both open the folded chairs and position them on either side of the dresser. Bobby asks him how they would determine who goes first, and Joey tells him that they had to flip a coin. Joey wins the coin toss and spins the gun. It lands on himself, so he takes his turn.

Then, Bobby spins the gun, and it lands on himself. He takes the gun and points it at his head, and it goes off. Joey was frantic! Seeing his buddy's head scattered all over the walls and ceiling, he could not handle the terrible sight and reality that Bobby was dead. With the other bullets that lay aside, Joey loads the gun again, points it at his chest, and takes his own life.

Tony was unaware of what was going on while in the front room. He turned down the television because he thought he heard a loud pop, and seconds later, it happened again. He then realized that it actually was a gunshot that he heard.

With no hesitation, he ran into the room that he heard the shots come from. Surprisingly, he saw Bobby's body on the floor and Joey's body was still in the chair slumped over. At this point, Tony is out of his mind. He somehow wants to satisfy his curiosity and see if Bobby was still alive. From his angle, he couldn't tell. Joey was gone for sure. Tony was crying the whole time and talking to himself. He goes over to Bobby to see if he was still breathing. When he found out that he was not, still out of his mind, he quickly ran out of the room and down the hall to the back door, stepping in a pool of blood as he exited. The blood was obviously on his shoe, and he could see it.

Tony ran out of the house at full speed and went to some wet grass and wiped off what blood he could off his sneakers.

He was not thinking rationally at all. As he ran out of the house, a neighbor of Joey's three houses down saw Tony flee from the house. It was about 8:30 pm and dark. At that time, the neighbor did not know why a black guy was running at a high rate of speed from the house. Tony went to a nearby park and called Vivian. When he began talking or attempting to talk, she could not make out what he was saying, not right away. He told her everything and that he would be home eventually and not to worry if she didn't see him right away; he would explain later.

Tony decided to stay in the park until late that night. Then, he would go back to the house and get his car, it's better this way. The next day, the police informed the public that there were two bodies found inside the home with bullet wounds. They also noticed shoe prints embedded with blood leading from the house to the grass outside. That could have or would have drawn a conclusion or a perception in the neighbor's mind that the black guy was a suspect and not a friend. Even though Tony had not done anything wrong, he understood that the possibility of being Stereotyped by society was almost a given. So it didn't matter if he attempted to explained his innocence, it would be invalid. So rather than go through this injustice, he decided to play it safe.

It's close to 8:00 am when he finally gets home. He tries with all his might not to show any emotions in front of the children. He tells Vivian to let them go to their rooms and close their doors because he had to talk to her. They had puzzled looks on their faces and had thoughts in their minds, of why their dad had not been home, but they did not dare ask. When they get in their rooms, he takes Vivian's hand and starts to cry uncontrollably again. It takes him awhile to maintain his composure, and is standing by his side crying as well, allowing him to get himself together. She kept telling him to breathe. She then went to the kitchen to get him something to drink and grabbed a few sheets of tissue on her way back. He got himself in the position to talk where she could understand him. He told her that the neighbor saw him leaving the house, and that most likely, the police would be looking for him. He told her that he could not believe what happened, and that he was still puzzled. The mystery of what happened to both of his brothers and the fact that they were dead was something that his emotions could not handle, he told her. Tony told Vivian to take the children over to her parents' house. She was reluctant at first, but he explained that this wouldn't be good for the children because they wouldn't understand, unlike adults.

"They are coming for me. I know, and I am completely innocent," he tells her. Tony was right. The police were looking for him using the description that they were given, to bring him in for questioning. Three hours later, three police cars pulled up in front of his house. Vivian and the children were long gone. They surround the house with guns drawn. One of the officers knocks on the door and asks if anyone was home. Tony does not hesitate to answer and tells him he is unarmed. He then opens the door. The officer tells him to show both of his hands and asks if anyone else is inside. He tells them that no one else was there. The officer then asks him what his first and last name was, and he tells him.

"You are the one we're looking for," one of the officers said. The officer allows him to lock the door and then tells him to turn around and put his hands behind him. The officer takes out his cuffs and puts them around his wrists and tells him he is under arrest for murder. Imagine what Tony must have been thinking at this time! He knew he was innocent but understood that this would have to take place. So with no resistance or hesitation, he went along peacefully. He tried to tell the officer that he had nothing to do with the murders he was referring to, but the officer did not believe him in the slightest.

Tony knew this as well. He just mentioned it because it sounded so cruel and the thought of him killing his buddies did not settle well in his mind. He was in denial for all the right reasons. The police took him to jail. They were already granted a warrant to search the house, but they had to take him into custody first. So they got in touch with Vivian, and she was instructed by the courts to meet the police at the house at a given time. They searched the entire house. They found a bag of clothes and sneakers under his bed. They took them to the forensics lab as evidence to be tested to see if any of the victim's blood was on them. The lab did not see any visible blood, so they used a fluorescent light to reveal any hidden blood if any. Well, they did discover some blood in the fibers on the side of the sneakers and some on the bottoms as well. This would now be admissible in court. They take him down to the precinct for booking. They then take him into the interrogation room.

A couple more hours passed, and Tony requested to speak to an attorney. By now, all of Rockford knew what happened, not with full detail, but the city was definitely aware. Tony called Vivian and asked her to get in touch with Bobby's grandfather. He knew that since Vivian had all the information, she could bring Phil up to speed. She tells Tony that she was ordered by the courts to go to the house and allowed the police to search the house. Tony was granted only one call. Tony was pretty clever when he thought this through, understanding that the one phone call was his lifeline. Since Vivian had most of the information, she could reach out to Phil, Bobby's grandfather.

Tony had two reasons for calling her. First, he did not have Phil's home or cell number. He didn't have to. He called Bobby all the time and had no reason to call Phil. Second he didn't have enough time to explain to Phil, the circumstances, if he did in fact get in touched with him. Vivian drove over to Phil's house. No one was at home at the time, so she left a note on the door for him to call her.

A couple of hours later, he calls her back. They agree to meet up, so she could update him and give him all of Tony's story and contact information at the jail. The reason Tony has reached out to Phil was because Phil has lived in Rockford for most of his life, about forty-six years of his life. Phil had a variety of friends and associates that he knew. Tony knows this, and if Phil doesn't have the answer to something, he will surely get one with all the resources he had at his disposal. Phil told Vivian to give him until the next day, and he would have an attorney who would talk with Tony. She shared with Tony everything that Phil had told her to keep him in the loop. Phil has a friend that happened to be an attorney that worked for the county. Phil called the attorney and told her what had happened. Unfortunately, she couldn't help.

The severity of the case would be tried in court on a state level, so she called one of her colleagues from the state and gave him the details about the case and told him that it was a personal referral. She also told him that she would still be a part of the defense team and let him know that the case was tried at the state level and needed him to argue the case, and she would assist him for the duration if he agreed to take the case.

The state representative asked what time and date the trial would start. He was told that he had two days before the trial began. She also told him not to worry. She would do all the legwork, which would save some time, and she would constantly communicate everything to him via cell phone or e-mail as she progressed, keeping him informed up to the minute. She kept Phil informed as well, but not with the details of which the team would argue. Their strategy would remain confidential for the team only. She contacted the jail and got more information from Tony firsthand.

Fortunately, the attorney agreed to take the case because he was in the middle of another case that was delayed. The duration of the other case was much longer which allowed him to argue Tony's case. Both attorneys had great rapport with one another. They had some history. They had previously tried cases together, not to mention the respect they have for each other. They both understood that if one should call the other in reference to any case, the reasons would be either because of the severity of a case or an issue of jurisdiction, which required their attention and in this case, that was exactly what had transpired.

After she talked to her colleague, he agreed. She called the jail again, letting Tony know that there was a team in place to represent him and to expect them to be there some time in the morning. Being in another part of the state, the state representative would have to catch a two-hour flight that same morning to meet with Tony so that they could collaborate and prep for the case. The state attorney quickly called the airlines and made reservations. It cost him more than the normal rate because of short notice. He then packed a couple of bags and his laptop, went to the bank, and got some cash. Remember, she kept him updated on everything doing all she could to conserve time. His cell phone constantly rang.

He arrives in Rockford at 9:00 am Tuesday morning. He rents a car at the airport and heads directly to the jail. She meets him there and they sign in. They get there and sign in. They are escorted to a room where Tony was waiting. They meet Tony for the first time. Tony reaches out his hand and introduces himself. His eyes are red and swollen, still not fully believing what actually happened. In return, the attorneys extend their hands and introduce themselves as well. The attorneys request to see their client in a more suitable room with no guards or staff members present. They are granted this request. The attorney tells Tony that he understands what has happened is not very common. He believes his story and assures him that if he hadn't then he would not have agreed to represent him. Tony goes on to tell the Attorney about his credentials, having a stable family, his appearance, his relationship with Bobby and Joey, and the fact that Phil has endorsed him. Phil has credibility and speaks highly of him, which says a great deal about Tony. The attorney tells Tony as long as he didn't sugarcoat or fabricate the story or withhold anything, he was confident that they would win the case.

Despite all the emotions, Tony feels a small amount of relief, a small grin shows up on his face. The attorney has an impressive resume and a high success rate of cases that he has tried.

His colleague has an impressive track record herself. Meanwhile, Phil calls Yvette and tells her what happened. While Phil was explaining what had happened, she was overwhelmed and dropped the phone, and Phil heard a loud scream as though someone was stabbing her in the chest. She never comes back to the phone, so her sister picks up the phone and continues the conversation with Phil. He gives her sister all the information and time of the funeral. He asks her sister to call him when Yvette came back to herself. He was concerned about her well-being.

Phil didn't have to call Yvette. She called him... in shock, she was worse off than Stacey. Phil gave her a few moments to get herself together. While he was doing that, she persistently asked why. He tried to calm her, but it was close to impossible. He simply told her that he was there for her, and he would text the information to her if she wanted to attend. A few days have passed. The funeral services were held during the same time as the trial. Tony found out when and where the services would take place, and when he did, he completely lost it, knowing he could not be there to pay his last respects to the two he loved dearly; just as much as he loved his children. The service was nice and respectable. Yvette and Stacey attended the funeral along with family, classmates, and friends.

CHAPTER 11

Inside the Courtroom
Day One!

The first day of court. The case is tried in front of a jury. The state has a system that preselects twelve jurors in the ready as there are so many cases. This system has worked for the state quite effectively. There are two sets of twelve, always ready with two alternates for each of the twelve on standby. They can be summoned within forty-eight hours to appear. This process is done by contacting them personally on their cell phones or e-mail. The potential Jurors have to check periodically to see if they have been assigned, until another twelve relieves them, then they rotate. This happens every three months.

It has been three days since Bobby and Joey have been dead. There is local and national news media everywhere. The nature of the crime brings in every walk of life. Bailiffs were situated at every entrance and exit and they were armed. The courtroom is full; most of the people from the funeral were in attendance including Stacey, Yvette, Vivian, his former boss, his parents, and his classmates.

Stacey notices that someone was crying frantically, so she made the assumption that this might be Yvette, Joey's girl. Stacey was still going through the emotions as well. She goes over to her and attempts to introduce herself while she tries very hard to contain herself. This was pretty obvious to people who didn't know either one of them that it was a possibility that they were the significant others. Both of them stood out among the crowd. Once they introduced themselves, they both embraced each other. Stacey sees Phil and his wife. Stacey tells Yvette that she was going to sit with Phil and that she was welcome to sit with them. Yvette tells her that she knows most of the people in the courtroom. She goes on to tell her that she grew up there, and she has a lot of support. Yvette grabs her hand and tells her thanks, but that she will be sitting with her family.

Before Yvette and Stacey part ways, Stacey asks her if she thought Tony had anything to do with the murders. Yvette responds by telling her no. And that she knew Tony for several years and has had many outings and functions that they both were a part of. She knew how close they all had been, and like any friends, they had small disagreements from time to time, but nothing major. So she further tells Stacey that something else had to have happened. Stacey embraces her again and tells her thanks and tells her if she needed anything, to call. She writes down her cell number and heads over to where Phil is sitting.

When she gets over to Phil and Susan, she embraces them. Stacey asks them also about Tony's innocence. Neither one of them believes he has committed the crime, but they went on to say that they too were curious to know what had happened that night when the trio were hanging out. As close as they all were, the curiosity was weighing down on all who knew their relationship. Most people did not think it was foul play.

There were a lot of familiar faces that Phil and Susan knew. They sat on the side of the defense. At this time, the head bailiff shouts out, "Court is in session. Everyone, be seated."

The courtroom gets very quiet. There's just a few sniffles that are heard. A couple of minutes pass, and two bailiffs bring Tony out of the back holding cell where he has been detained. The entire courtroom looks in his direction, sighing as he enters. His wife abruptly leaves for the bathroom, not being able to handle seeing him in his current condition. He is wearing a white jumpsuit with his last name on it along with the letters ICU, Illinois Correctional Unit. He has shackles on his hands and feet and you can hear them with every step he takes. He also has a covering over his mouth, so he would not spit on the crowd if he chose. This was unfortunate for him.

The state had labeled him as a hardened criminal. After they sit him down, they take off the protective mask. Not long after, he turns around and blows a kiss at his wife, then looks at Phil and Susan and whispers (thank you). He then turns back around and shakes the hands of both of his defense attorneys.

The head bailiff yells out again, "Attention! All rise, The Honorable Judge Perkins is presiding."

The judge walks toward the bench with a folder in his hand. He pulls out his chair and sits down, glances at the crowd, pours himself a glass of water, and puts on his reading glasses.

He then opens the folder and announces the *State vs. Tony Moore*, the date, the time, the case number, and the courtroom number. The defense, the state (prosecution), and the jurors all got out of their seats and faced the front of the bench, including Tony. When the judge was finished with the announcements, the bailiff asked everyone to sit down. The judge looks at the prosecution and tells them to start with the opening arguments.

The prosecution starts out with showing the evidence, at first trying to pray on the jury's emotions, hoping that they could get a quick conviction, just by confirming that blood that was on Tony's sneakers was not his, and it had belonged to one of the victims. The prosecution called the representative from the forensics lab to testify and back up the confirmation. Before the prosecution asked the representative to make a confirmation, he wanted her to state her name and state the field she was in; she made mention of her credentials, where she studied, how many degrees she had, how many years of study and years of practice in her field. She had to prove her credibility in case the defense wanted to argue her credibility. The prosecution wanted to establish this early on. She told the jury that there was no visible blood, so she used another method to discover the blood if there was any. They did in fact find blood on the side of the sneakers and in the crevice's on the bottom of the sneakers. Tony's eyes bulged out of his head. He thought that he cleaned off all the blood. It didn't dawn on him that the blood could be in the fabric on the side and in the crevices on the bottom of the sneakers.

The defense was definitely taking notes. The prosecution says that the evidence on the shoes was one of the things that they would be addressing to build a conviction. Most of the crowd raised eyebrows when the prosecutors presented the first evidence, thinking what could become of this. There was no doubt there because the defense did not counter or argue the opposition, so it was confirmed. The prosecutor displayed his ego by looking at the jurors, making a statement to reassure them that Tony will get what's coming to him.

The judge objects and tells him not to draw conclusions and to move on with his arguments, way before the defense could respond… they were just about to do so. The prosecutor continues to prove his case. He brings up the fact that Tony's DNA was found inside the house on several pieces of furniture. It was also found on the refrigerator, the back-door handle, the television remote, and a couple of beer bottles. Forensics report confirms it. The prosecution then brings up the neighbor who saw him flee the house. They call the neighbor to the stand. After she is sworn in, they ask her a series of questions, her name, age, and how long she lived in her home, etc. One of the questions was could she identify the person who was leaving the house. She replied that she could, so the prosecutor asked her to point to him, and she pointed to Tony.

The judge then asks the defense if they wanted to cross-examine the witness. Yes, they did, so they asked the witness how dark it might have been and asked about the condition of her eyes. The witness confirmed that it was dark, but there was a streetlight that made Tony's appearance clear and had no issues with her sight. She went on to say that she could prove it with optometry records if she needed to. The defense did not think this was necessary, so the defense rests for the moment. Then, the judge asks both sides if they have any more questions for the witness. Both sides say no.

The judge then asks the witness to step down and tells the prosecution to proceed. The prosecutor insinuates how crime is high in certain areas and not in others, there are certain retail shops (swap meets a.k.a. flea markets), liquor stores, pawnshops, stating that certain things happen in certain cultures. He further states there are a particular number of people that are already incarcerated and have lots of children. The defense recognizes those accusations and quickly objects.

The judge agrees and warns him again of his shrewd demeanor. The prosecutor then changes the subject. The prosecutor tells the jury that he doesn't understand why Tony was at the house in the first place. He puts a lot of emphasis on this. The prosecution closes by saying if the blood that was on his shoes aren't evidence enough, then what is? "Furthermore, "the proof is in the pudding" and how much more convincing must take place before they make the determination that this criminal had committed this horrific crime. If the jury doesn't convict him, they will be allowing his kind to roam free."

The crowd reacts, not liking the remarks that the prosecutor was giving. Neither did the defense nor the judge. The defense once again objects and tells the judge he's doing it again. The judge faces the prosecution and tells him that if he has one more derogatory statement while the trial was in session, they will be in contempt of court and have to pay a fine, no more warnings. The prosecution rests for now. The judge turns and looks at the defense and tells them that they can start their opening arguments.

The defense starts off talking about Tony's character. They start off telling the jury how he had no prior criminal records. They mention that he was a family man and how much he was involved with his children, both socially and emotionally.

The defense calls Vivian to the stand so that she can tell the jury how involved he is with his children. She is sobbing the whole time that she is approaching the witness stand, she even stops on occasion, wiping her face with tissue. They ask her a question about how involved he was. She answers the court by saying he goes to the PTA meetings every chance he gets if he is not working. He keeps up with their grades and corrects them if necessary. He goes to just about all their sporting events if he doesn't have to work long hours. During spring and summer vacations, he takes them to amusement parks, zoos, picnics, church, museums occasionally and fishing. When the family isn't traveling, he is always involved in some form or fashion. The defense thanks her for answering the questions.

The judge asks the prosecutor if he would like to cross-examine. They do. They ask if he is involved with their grades, "what kind of grades do they get?"

Vivian looks up at the prosecutor with a disgusted face and says, "What kind of damn grades do you think they get, Mr. Prosecutor?"

And Tony replies, "Exactly!" although he's not supposed to. The judge steps in and tells them both that he understands how their emotions have been stirred up, but he asks them to try to conduct themselves. The prosecutor has no more questions for the witness. The defense tells the judge that they have another question for the witness. The judge tells them to proceed. So they ask her to tell them about Tony's education, trying to establish that he is not the typical stereotype.

Vivian tells the jury that he was motivated to take up the electrical trade and join an electrical apprenticeship school, how he has completed the four-year school and graduated with an impressive GPA. He was awarded perfect attendance three of the four years that he was enrolled there. She went further to say that the graduation ceremony was a dignified event. Having to walk the stage and receive his certification that was endorsed by the US Department of Labor and several of their colleagues and representatives, says a lot. Last, she told them how he started his career and was offered a position of general foreman, making about seventy to eighty-five thousand a year, to provide for his family. When asked if she thinks Tony committed the crime, she told them, "No! He did not kill those two!"

The judge asked the defense if they had any more questions for her. They said no, they didn't. The judge thanked her and asked her to step down. The defense continues, focusing on the relationship they had. He tells the jury that Joey, Bobby and Tony had a compelling history. How they used to stay the night at one another's houses, rotating every now and again. (How they all would experience the different types of food they would eat despite their cultures.) The trio had a friendship like no other. It was rare to say the least. The compassion they had for each other at an early age was even more intriguing. Falling short of being biological brothers, they were brothers nonetheless. The defense told them how the three would have an occasional skirmish with others if anyone violated them, going on to say they backed each other, no matter the cost. Continuing his arguments, he stated how Bobby's parents lost their lives in a plane crash while on vacation. They all rallied together to comfort Bobby in his time of need (they were in middle school at that time). Both Tony and Joey stayed with Bobby as long as they were allowed. The days that they had school were cut short, but the weekends were entirely different.

The defense went on telling them about life in high school, how they all came together during breakups with their girlfriends, the time Tony and his football team lost the biggest game of the year as seniors, never to play in that particular game again and how they supported him. All were in attendance when Joey and Bobby went to the armed forces. They supported and encouraged each other while enjoying a home-cooked meal and a few drinks as they temporarily parted ways.

"In my honest opinion, it doesn't appear that a relationship such as this one would cause Tony to do something malicious to the very people that he loved dearly," the defense said.

The jury was amazed at this and were definitely taking notes. It's about 4:50 pm. The judge tells the defense that they could continue tomorrow, commencing at 9:00 am he then adjourned the court.

The bailiff yells, "Court is now adjourned and will resume at 9:00 am tomorrow."

The bailiff escorts the judge to his chambers first, and then they take Tony back to the holding cell. The defense can visit Tony at any time during the hours of 7:00 am up until 8:00 pm Monday through Friday if they choose, for the briefing, information, strategy, comments, support, anything that involves the client or the case itself. So they meet with Tony for a while to bring him up to speed on how they intend on pursuing the case and the direction in which they are headed. They also ask him for his input as the case proceeds.

CHAPTER 12

Inside the Courtroom
Day Two!

It's 9:00 am, the second day of the trial and the fourth day Joey and Bobby have been dead. The defense is still building their case. They call several character witnesses to the stand to continue to build up Tony's character. The witnesses were called at various times throughout the day. The witnesses talked about how they personally experienced or have seen different circumstances or trials that have played out in the lives of the trio. There were people from high school, middle school, and even as far back as elementary school. Some were related to Bobby and some Joey. Some were old customers from the store. Some were old classmates, etc.

Twenty minutes before the trial began, Tony's old boss Mr. Sherman asked the defense if they would put him on the stand. He wanted to tell the jury more about Tony and his credibility. The team then asks Tony if he is OK with putting Mr. Sherman on the stand. He agreed, so they allowed this. He was called to the stand as opening arguments were resumed by the defense. He was warned that the prosecutor might possibly ask him some questions of their own. Mr. Sherman had tossed and turned all night wondering how he could be a part of Tony's defense. He figured that giving detailed testimony of how they worked well together and how he was a big contributor to the store's success would have some bearing on the case. He also didn't like the fact that Tony was shackled like an animal.

All the previous witnesses had given their testimonies. It was time for Mr. Sherman's. The courageous sixty-eight-year-old man was called to the stand by the defense. The whole time on the stand, he was looking at Tony and the jury periodically, sobbing the entire time. He starts off by saying how much ambition and determination he had, to be something in life. He was responsible and was willing to work and he loved to help people. He went on to say how Tony was eager to learn as he would show him how to manage the store. He was a good listener and would do anything that you asked of him.

Mr. Sherman turns to Tony and tells him that he turned out to be a good man and gave him a salute. You could hear the emotions of the crowd. Most of them anyway. The sixty-eight-year-old then took off his glasses and put his head down. The judge asked him if he was OK and instructed the bailiff to bring Mr. Sherman some tissue. Then, the judge told him to take his time, and when he was ready, he could step down. The judge then asked the prosecutor if he wanted to cross examine. The prosecution then rested. The judge then asked the defense if they had anything further to add. They declined. The judge then instructs the prosecution to start with closing arguments.

They start off again, putting emphasis on the blood that was found on Tony's sneakers, which is proof enough to convict him. The gun that was found at the scene could not be used as evidence because it had blood all over it, and the forensics lab could not retrieve fingerprints off it because of the blood. The sneakers, the matching shoe patterns found inside and out of the house, and the witnessing of the neighbor were the only credible things that could be used.

The prosecution admits that Tony has proven that he is a great person and has contributed to society.

Admitting that the testimonies were consistent with one another, showed worthiness, stating that it's all great. If he went on that alone, he would be innocent, but that's not how it works. However, he had to prove his case on the evidence and that alone. Continuing, he said something had to happen inside that house nonetheless. "So we are left with that on our minds. Unfortunately, Bobby or Joey are not with us to testify. It's not to be taken personally or to be taken lightly. My job is to convict a person if the evidence is consistent with the crime committed. Furthermore, I would hope that he is innocent. He seems to be a great person in the eyes of many. I was wrong to pass judgment and easily stereotype," he went on to say. The prosecution completed their closing arguments.

Meanwhile, the assistant to the defense attorney looked over at her colleague and whispered to him that the prosecutor has not said anything about gunpowder in any way. She suggested that Tony or his clothes had not been tested, and if there is gunpowder on him or his clothes, that would suggest that he had something to do with the shooting in some form or fashion. He whispered back to her and said that was exactly right, stating that; that was a good observation, while he took down notes.

At this time, the judge instructs the defense to start their closing arguments. He stands up and heads over to the jury box. He acknowledges that there is visible blood on his client's sneakers merely because he went over to one of the victims to check and see if they were still alive. They contend that this is a normal reaction. Taking into consideration that there was nothing mentioned about the gunpowder, he tells this to the judge and asks him if he could postpone the trial another day before the jury reached a verdict. He also requests that Tony's clothes and shoes are examined again this time for gunpowder residue by the forensics lab. Tony's clothes were held in a secure place for evidence, and only the judge could request to retrieve items that were placed in this secure place. If anyone tampered with any of the items, it was considered a felony and could face up to ten years in prison, depending on the importance of that particular item.

The judge agrees and it's close to 2:30 pm. He instructs the head bailiff to announce an adjournment until noon the next day. This would give the lab time to examine the clothing. The judge then goes into his chamber and makes a couple of phone calls; one to the department that holds the evidence and the other to the forensics lab. The lab receives the request from the judge and starts working immediately, working late into the evening. The defense meets up with Tony that night as well bringing him up to speed on their intentions and the approach they will be taking. They asked him if he has any input that may be valuable.

The crowd that's in favor of the defense goes home with some relief, but still remained optimistic until the trial was over. After the defense attorney's part ways with Tony, they both go back to her office and prepare for what's coming tomorrow. They stay up late, taking advantage of the time that the judge has allowed. They order pizza for the night. They search the Web, looking for all things associated with gunpowder, educating themselves. They take more notes and discuss their strategy. The forensics lab contacts the judge at about 10:00 am the next day and tells him that they have the results of the clothing and sneakers, suggesting that they check Tony's skin as well.

The tech told the judge that she has a kit that she could bring to court and conduct the testing there, as long as he would allow it, stating that the test would only take fifteen minutes. The judge agrees. He requests the same person that conducted the first test to take the witness stand when court began, so she could explain her findings to the court and all that were in attendance. Court wouldn't start for another couple of hours.

The defense arrives at the courthouse at 10:30 am. They meet with Tony for the last time before heading inside the courtroom. They brought donuts, coffee, and milk with them as they visit with him, getting permissions from the guards of course; telling him that they stayed up late preparing. Tony is pleased with what he hears and is very grateful for the donuts and their involvement in his defense.

Twelve o'clock noon, court is now in session. The bailiffs announce, "All rise!" as the Judge enters the courtroom. He sits down at the bench and tells the court that the defense will continue with closing arguments. The Judge lets them know that the results are in from the forensics lab. The lead tech will take the stand first, before the defense proceeds; to share the results with everyone in the courtroom so that everyone will be informed simultaneously. He says that the prosecution can cross-examine if they choose because the witness is asked to take the stand for a different time and for a different reason since the issue of gunpowder came into play, although both sides have had their closing arguments.

The judge calls both of the attorneys to the bench and tells them about the test that will be conducted by forensics and the duration of the test. Both parties go back to their respective sides and share the information with their teams.

The bailiff calls her to the stand once more and swears her in. She starts off saying that they checked both the sneakers and the clothes of Tony Moore and found out that there was no evidence of gunpowder on either one when they conducted testing at the lab. She told the court that they will be checking his skin as well, and this will be conducted inside the courtroom.

Before the tech administers the test, she explains to the court that if he had gunpowder on him, then it would show. She went on to explain that if gunpowder was present, it would stay on the skin for seven days, and it would stay on clothing for six months. The judge asks her if she had explained everything pertinent or pertaining to the gunpowder that she may have left out, before they moved forward with the testing. He then asks both the prosecutor and the defense if they had any questions. Neither side had any questions. The judge then asks her to step down off the witness stand and proceed with the testing. She grabs her test kit and heads over to Tony. She explains to him exactly what she'll be doing as she conducts the testing. After she puts on her latex gloves, she has him extend his arms and applies a special type of lotion on his arms and both sides of his hands. She then applies a special powder, similar with baby powder, sprinkling it on his skin while the lotion is still wet. She waits for fifteen minutes for any visible signs of gunpowder.

Fifteen minutes passed, and there were no signs. She wipes off the excess lotion, takes her things, and walks back to the stand. The judge then asks the prosecutor if he has any further questions for the tech. He stated that something did come to mind, so he asked the tech, "The testing that was done at the lab, how accurate is it?"

The tech replied that it was very accurate. In fact, they have to, by law, have another tech confirm the findings. If this was not done, then the techs could lose their licenses and possibly serve time in jail. She had the report with her and the names and information of all the techs who were involved, their signatures and dates of examinations at their disposal.

The prosecutor requests a copy and then rests his case. The judge then asks the defense to close before they turn it over to the jury.

The defense asks the following question, "So that we understand, there are no traces of gunpowder on his skin or clothing and the fact that this is the fifth day that the victims have passed away. Would it be safe to say that my conclusion suggests that my client is well under the grace period of seven days?"

The tech answers, "Yes."

He then looks over at his team and smiles. Closing, he goes on to say that with necessary testing that the lab has conducted required by the courts and the character witnesses that have come forward, the defense is convinced that these two things combined will acquit their client. However, they also understand that the jury had to make the final determination of his fate. The defense thanks the jury and the judge and rests its case. The judge then instructs the jury to deliberate and then calls a recess for lunch. Remember, court commenced at noon, so they had a late lunch to begin with. The duration of the lunches are normally one hour long. Lunch started at 4:00 pm and was over at 5:30 pm. The Jury has lunch as they deliberate, they ordered sandwiches and chips from the local sandwich deli to avoid going out.

It's 5:30 pm, and everyone is back in the courtroom. The bailiff calls the court to order and acknowledges the judge as he approaches the bench. The jury re-enters the courtroom; the foreman is leading them. It takes them only forty-five minutes to deliberate. The judge asks the jury to remain standing. He announces two counts of homicide in the first degree, "The *State of Illinois vs. Tony Moore* accused of homicide case number 1110912, May 14, 2003. He announces this for the court reporter to record. Then, he asks the foreman to read the verdict aloud.

The foreman reads, "We have found the defendant Tony Moore not guilty and innocent of all charges that were alleged."

The courtroom shouts, most of them anyway. The judge announces that he was free to go and slams his gavel on the bench. The judge goes over to Tony and congratulates him, making reference to his character and making contributions to the community. He also told him that he was fortunate because he has tried a lot of similar cases, and some were not so lucky, and that he was proven worthy. He pats Tony on the shoulder and wishes him well. Tony puts his hands over his eyes and puts his head down on the table in front of him. He is overwhelmed with all types of emotion; as though someone had stuck one hundred knives in him all at once.

A few days had passed since the trials. Tony wants to pay respects to his two friends, so he visits the cemetery where they lie to rest. Bobby and Joey are buried side by side. Tony walks over to both tombstones and kneels down. He makes a sincere statement while talking to them. "Hey, my brothers, nothing came to mind that was more important to me than these mini-skateboards. I leave them with you so we can forever be bonded together. As I constructed them, I wanted to show complete solidarity as I put every piece together giving thought to the wonderful life we all shared. I love you both. I will be there for your families no matter the cost. Rest in peace my brothers... May God be with you both." He places the skateboards down in front of each tombstone and blows each one a kiss. He is filled with so much emotion he could hardly walk. He turns around and slowly walks back to his car in the same direction that the sun is setting.

ABOUT THE AUTHOR

Anthony S., a.k.a. Tone, was born in Los Angeles, California, in 1966. He has been married to the love of his life, Cheryl, for twenty-plus years. The author's mom, Datie (Dee), has always encouraged him, and the spirit of his father, who they lost in 2015, has also encouraged him to move forward. He has three grown children who he loves dearly: Charnell, Marvin, and Toniqua. Anthony is also proud to say that he has two beautiful grandchildren, Israel and Immanuel. He has three brothers, Cliff, Rodney, and Yancy, and one sister, Duffy. Through the years, the author has lived in northern Illinois and eventually moved to north Texas where he currently resides. He loves to write. He has been inspired by many, but he says that he has received his ultimate inspiration from God himself who strengthens and sustains him. This is the author's first novel.

Author name/Pen name "Anthony S." (AKA)

CPSIA information can be obtained
at www.ICGtesting.com
Printed in the USA
BVHW03*1928290618
520468BV00003B/26/P

9 781633 387560